"You could take your dress off," Hugh offered helpfully.

"Yes, I could," she reflected aloud.

And damned if she didn't!

Right then. Right there.

Well, actually it took a few moments for her to get the dress off. Palm-dampening, mouth-parching, body-hardening moments as far as Hugh was concerned. Soaking wet and clingy beaded dresses were obviously not easy to shed.

But as he stood there gaping, the crazy woman peeled the silvery straps of her beaded dress right down her arms and wriggled and shimmied and squirmed until the dress pooled at her feet and she was wearing a strapless bra and a pair of itsy-bitsy teeny-weeny bikini panties and nothing more.

Harlequin Presents® is proud to bring you
a brand-new trilogy from international
bestselling author

ANNE McALLISTER

Welcome to

The McGillivrays of Pelican Cay

Meet:
Lachlan McGillivray—he's ready to take his
pretend mistress to bed!
Hugh McGillivray—is about to claim a bride....
Molly McGillivray—her Spanish lover is ready
to surrender to passion!

Visit:
The stunning tropical island of Pelican Cay—
full of sun-drenched beaches,
it's the perfect place for passion!

Don't miss this fantastic trilogy:
McGillivray's Mistress—November 2003
In McGillivray's Bed—July 2004

And coming soon in Harlequin Presents®
Molly's story

Anne McAllister

IN McGILLIVRAY'S BED

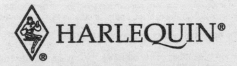

TORONTO • NEW YORK • LONDON
AMSTERDAM • PARIS • SYDNEY • HAMBURG
STOCKHOLM • ATHENS • TOKYO • MILAN • MADRID
PRAGUE • WARSAW • BUDAPEST • AUCKLAND

For James, with love

In memory of Belle,
always the best

ISBN 0-373-12406-6

IN McGILLIVRAY'S BED

First North American Publication 2004.

www.eHarlequin.com

Printed in U.S.A.

CHAPTER ONE

IT WASN'T exactly heaven.

It sure as heck wasn't Iowa.

But it was as close as he was ever likely to get to perfection, Hugh McGillivray decided as he lounged back in the chair on his gently rocking boat, playing out his hand line, hoping for one last catch as he lazed away the end of the day in the setting Caribbean sun.

At the stern another rod bobbed in its holder, increasing his odds. But even if he didn't get any more fish, Hugh didn't care. It had still been a perfect day. The sort of idyllic day he remembered from childhood—where anything could happen or nothing could—and each was equally welcome.

They were the days he'd dreamed about during his years as a Navy pilot when rules and regulations and spit and polish had ruled his every waking hour. They were the days he'd been determined to enjoy again. They were the reason he'd left the Navy five years ago and come home to start up Fly Guy, his island charter business on tiny laid-back Pelican Cay.

Most days flying passengers and cargo kept him busy moving among the islands and to the coastal cities of the States. Most days he was delighted to do it—enjoying the variety of people he met and places he went and jobs he took.

"Never a dull moment," he'd told his brother Lachlan cheerfully last week.

But that wasn't precisely true.

Some days—some *wonderful* days—no one wanted to go

anywhere, no one wanted to send anything, things were dull as ditch water. And Hugh loved those days even more because on those days he was totally free.

Like today, he thought, smiling and flexing his shoulders, then jiggling his hand line just a bit, wiggling his toes and relishing the beauty of the sunset and the soft sea breeze that ruffled his hair.

Of course, he could have been back at the shop helping his sister, Molly, work on the chopper engine or he could have been doing his paperwork or sending out his bills.

But the papers and the bills would be there tomorrow. So would Molly. And she'd be a damn sight happier for not having had him underfoot today. They were good friends most of the time—partners for the past four years; Molly did most of the mechanic work and Hugh did most of the flying—but they came close to strangling each other whenever they worked together on the same project.

So it had been the wisest thing, he assured himself, not to mention the safest, considering Molly's proverbial redhead's temper, to wave her goodbye this morning, whistle up his border collie, Belle, and head out for a day's fishing.

He'd done some bottom fishing early, checking out several favorite spots. Then, long about lunchtime, he'd dropped anchor at a little cove on Pistol Island, a few miles east of Pelican Cay. There he'd eaten his bologna sandwiches and drunk a couple of beers while Belle had explored the mangroves and then went swimming. After Hugh had swum a bit, too, he'd begun working his way back toward Pelican Cay, though *work* hardly seemed the operative word.

Mostly he just fiddled with his lines, soaked up the rays, sipped his beer and drifted along as the sun dropped into the sea.

He watched with mild interest as speedboats zipped past him. But he felt no urge to move quicker. If he wanted speed, he flew. Today he wanted to drift. He'd waved at the launch taking the day-trippers back to Nassau from

Pelican Cay when it had passed him a couple of hours ago. The passengers had waved back, looking tired and sunburned but, he supposed, happy.

No happier than he was, though.

No one was happier than Hugh McGillivray in his battered wooden boat—not even those high-living folks he'd seen partying on the snazzy yacht that had cruised past just a little while ago. He could still hear the sounds of calypso floating his way and see its lights in the dusk heading northwest.

He reached into his cooler and pulled out one last beer. The cooler had been full of ice and beer and sandwiches when he'd left this morning. Now it was full of fish—on top of what ice was left. He had enough fish to last all week and enough to share the largesse with Molly and Lachlan and Fiona, Lachlan's wife.

He'd been hoping for a good-size grouper—one that would top the fish Lachlan had brought home last week. They'd been competing since they had come to Pelican Cay as teenagers. Lachlan still held the all-time record—having landed a fifty-eight-pound grouper when he was nineteen. But that had been half a lifetime ago. And even though he'd been insisting since then that Hugh would never beat him, Hugh still figured he would.

Especially now that Lachlan rarely went fishing anymore. He was far too busy these days with his collection of small inns and resort hotels, not to mention with his wife. Particularly now that Fiona was expecting.

Hugh grinned as he thought of his normally svelte sister-in-law who was now in what she called "the waddling way." Fiona had been his friend for a lot of years. He thought she'd make a wonderful mom. The thought of Lachlan as a dad boggled the mind. Actually the thought of Lachlan as a husband had taken some getting used to. During his years as a professional soccer player, Lachlan had been known in the tabloids as "the gorgeous goalie," and he'd certainly taken advantage of his reputation.

Women had followed him in droves. Probably still would follow him if he showed any interest.

But Lachlan was only interested in Fiona. These days the gorgeous goalie was as domesticated as a cat.

Hugh wasn't.

Ever since Carin Campbell had married Nathan Wolfe two years ago, Hugh had decided that confirmed bachelorhood had a lot to recommend it. At the time he'd been seriously miffed that Carin had chosen another man—not that he'd shown it. He'd never ever worn his heart on his sleeve where Carin was concerned.

No one knew how much he'd cared.

Privately, though, Hugh had made up his mind that since the only woman worth marrying was taken, from here on out he'd simply play the field.

It wasn't a bad deal. He could still admire Carin—love Carin, he admitted to himself—and enjoy her friendship. But he could also sidle up to any interesting female who turned up on Pelican Cay and flirt a little bit.

Or a lot. Whatever the situation required.

Hugh enjoyed flirting almost as much as he enjoyed fishing. It was fun. It sometimes led to bed which was also fun. And as long as no one took it seriously, no one got hurt.

He wished Lisa Milligan didn't take it so seriously.

The flirting bit. Not the bed bit. They'd got to the flirting. They hadn't got to bed—and they weren't going to.

It was against his principles. Hugh was quite happy to go to bed with willing women who knew they were having fun and nothing more. He wasn't about to sleep with any woman who thought she was going to haul him to the altar.

And he didn't need to be a mind reader to know that's exactly what Lisa had in mind.

Lisa Milligan was a sweet naive young girl. *Girl* being the operative word. She was nineteen, for God's sake! A child! Well, perhaps slightly more than that. But not much.

She was Tony at the bakery's niece, taking a break from

college and working on the front desk at the Mirabelle, Lachlan's extremely upscale, ultradiscreet, very fashionable Pelican Cay inn. She'd been there since spring.

Finding herself, she told him.

Mostly, Hugh thought grimly, finding *him.*

In the beginning he'd teased and flirted with her a bit because it was what he did. That didn't mean he wanted to marry her.

Lisa just thought it did. In fact she *expected* he would marry her. Like it was a foregone conclusion. She'd told Miss Saffron, the island's biggest gossip, exactly that.

"She say it only be a matter of time," Miss Saffron had told him a while back as she'd rocked on the swing of her shady front porch.

Not in this lifetime, Hugh had thought, shaken. He'd been doing his best to steer clear of Lisa ever since.

But it hadn't helped. Nothing had helped. Not even when he'd told her flat out that he wasn't the marrying kind.

She'd just laughed and shown him her incredible dimples, then flashed her gorgeous grin. "Then I'll just have to change your mind."

She'd been doing her best for the past month. Everywhere Hugh had gone, there she'd been. In his shop, at the landing pad, on the dock, in the hammock on his porch this morning, for heaven's sake!

"I wondered if you wanted to go for a swim?" she'd said hopefully.

"Can't." He'd been polite but brisk. It was a small island. People had to get along. He didn't want to hurt her feelings. He just wanted her to understand she wasn't for him.

"Oh." She'd looked crestfallen. "I'll see you later, then?"

He'd grunted. "Gonna be gone all day."

"I could come along. It's my day off."

He'd shaken his head. "Sorry. It's business."

Stretching the truth, perhaps. Molly would have called

him a liar. But he wasn't. He needed to know where the good fishing was, didn't he? That way he could direct his clients who wanted to know where to drop their lines.

He'd been taking care of business all day, enjoying every moment with only Belle, his dog, for company. He especially enjoyed the fact that the entire landscape was Lisa-free.

Now Hugh stretched expansively, lounged back and, one last time before he headed home, jiggled his line.

It jiggled back.

"Whoa." He sat up straight and grinned, patience rewarded. He played the line out a little, then drew it in, testing to be sure he hadn't simply snagged a piece of driftwood.

He got a responding twitch. The twitch became a tug. A strong tug.

Hugh laughed delightedly. No driftwood this! Whistling through his teeth, he began hauling it in.

"Look at that!" he said happily to Belle when it jerked hard against his hand. "We've got a live one."

The dog opened one eye and looked mildly interested, then started to close it again when the rod behind Hugh began to jerk and rattle as well.

Startled, Hugh swiveled around to see it bending and rocking like mad in the twilight as Belle jumped up and barked at it. "Hang on." He reached to grab it, too, just as he caught sight of a thrashing movement off the side of the boat.

One hell of a *big* thrashing movement. The line he held jerked hard and he wrapped it quickly and tightly around his hand.

What in God's name had he caught? A bloody whale?

He braced his feet and began to haul it in again when all of a sudden his catch broke the surface.

A *woman*—an absolutely furious woman—sputtered up. "For heaven's sake, stop yanking on that line! You're going to rip my dress right off!"

Hugh goggled.

A *woman?*

He'd caught *a woman?*

No. Not possible. He gave his heat-baked brain a quick hard shake.

But even as he doubted and wondered if he'd had too much sun and too many beers, the line jerked in his hand, the rod bobbed madly and Belle leaned eagerly over the edge and wagged her tail and barked.

So she was real.

He wasn't seeing things.

It was a woman. Or a...*mermaid?*

His mind wouldn't even go there.

"Shut up, you stupid dog," he muttered. Then, "Stop thrashing around," he snapped at the woman.

"I'm *not* thrashing," she retorted furiously. "I'm trying to get this damn hook out!" And abruptly she disappeared underwater leaving Hugh to stare at the empty ocean in the sudden silence and doubt his sanity once more.

Belle whined and leaned precariously over the edge. Hugh grabbed her collar and hauled her back just as the woman bobbed up again and the line jerked furiously in his hand, meaning she hadn't got the hook out.

"Damned beaded dresses," she said with annoyance.

Beaded dresses?

Hugh's jaw sagged. But he could see that she did appear to be wearing something with sparkly silver straps over her shoulders. A beaded dress? Who the hell went swimming in a beaded dress?

She gave one more futile yank, then stopped fighting with the hook and took a couple of overhand strokes, which brought her closer to the boat but tangled her even further with his lines.

"Do you have a knife?" she demanded.

Did fish swim in the sea? "Of course I've got a knife."

"Then give it here. Or cut the line and pull me out," she ordered, stretching out a hand and sounding like

Barrett, his old commanding officer, the one they'd called Captain Ahab behind his back because he was as irrational and stubborn as Melville's legendary captain.

Barrett—and Ahab—had nothing on this woman. If she'd acted the least bit desperate, he would have handed over his knife in an instant. But he was damned if he was taking orders from a bossy mermaid.

"Well?" she demanded impatiently when he didn't move. "What are you waiting for?"

"The magic word?" he drawled, raising one brow.

"Oh, for heaven's sake!" She began kicking again, splashing him.

"You might not want to do that," he suggested. "You'll attract sharks."

Her eyes widened. "There aren't—"

"Of course there are," he said. "Big ones. Hungry ones. In case," he added, "you thought *Jaws* was just a movie." He cocked his head, and smiled at her, all the while thinking this was the most surreal experience he'd ever had in his life.

Belle whined and peered over the side.

The woman looked from him to his dog and back again. She pressed her lips together tightly, then rolled her eyes and shrugged, nearly sinking as she did so. Then she muttered a less than gracious, "Please."

"By all means," Hugh said affably and nudging Belle out of the way, grasped the woman's outstretched hand and pulled. As she came out of the water, he got both of her hands, and she floundered, kicking and slithering, and landed against him, cold and wet as a fish.

But she didn't feel like a fish.

She felt like 100 percent woman with soft breasts and shapely hips. And feet.

He felt both relieved—and irritated—that she had feet.

"What the hell were you doing out there swimming around in the middle of the damn ocean?" he demanded, gripping her arms.

She twisted out of his grasp and shoved away to stand on her own. Then she shook long wet dark hair out of her eyes and glared at him. "Well, I wasn't swimming laps. I was trying to reach your boat obviously!"

"*My* boat?" That hadn't even occurred to him.

"Your *boat*." She corrected his emphasis. "It was the closest thing to aim for," she explained as if he were slightly dim-witted.

Hugh didn't think that under the circumstances *he* was the one whose wits needed questioning.

But he had a notion now where she'd come from. He arched a brow and looked her up and down, taking in the sparkly beaded dress that ended just above very shapely knees and outlined extremely enticing curves. A very snazzy cocktail dress. Not exactly day-tripper wear. More ritzy party girl. She could only have fallen off the yacht whose running lights he could still see far off in the distance.

"What happened?" he asked her. "Drink too much? Get a little tipsy? Lose your footing?"

"What?" She looked at him, offended.

So he spelled it out. "Fall off the yacht, sweetheart?"

"I did not fall off the yacht," she told him flatly, lifting a chin not unlike Captain Ahab's chin. "I jumped."

Hugh's jaw dropped. *"You what!"*

"I jumped," she repeated calmly, which was exactly what he couldn't believe she'd said the first time.

"Are you crazy? You *jumped?* In the middle of the bloody ocean? What the hell did you do a stupid thing like that for?"

The crazy woman drew herself up as tall as she could manage, which meant she was almost as tall as he was, and looked down her definitely Captain Ahab nose. "It was," she informed him, "the proactive thing to do."

Hugh sputtered. *"Proactive?"*

How like a ditsy female to use business babble to justify temporary insanity. At least he hoped it was temporary. He jerked his baseball cap off, ran a hand through his hair, jammed it back on again and shook his head.

"You don't have to be embarrassed just because you drank a bit too much," he told her. "Lots of people get a little wasted when they have a day's holiday."

But her chin just went higher. "It wasn't a holiday. And I did not touch a drop. I never drink on business occasions."

"You jump often?" Hugh inquired. "On business occasions?" His mouth twitched.

She gave him a fulminating glare, then wrapped her arms around her dripping dress and scowled. "Fine. Don't believe me. I don't care. It doesn't matter to me whether you believe me or not." Pause. "But I would appreciate a towel."

He didn't move.

The scowl grew deeper, the glare more intense. Their eyes dueled. Then Miss Captain Ahab pressed her lips together tightly. There was a long pause. Finally she gave an irritable huff and added with bad grace, "Please."

Hugh grinned. "Coming right up!"

He fished a not-very-clean towel out from beneath the bow of the boat where he always stowed his sleeping bag and cooler and other sundry gear and tossed it back to her. "It's all yours."

She caught it, wiped her face, then met his gaze over the top of it. "Thank you," she said with exaggerated politeness.

Still grinning, he dipped his head. "Anytime."

She looked away then and began drying off. Hugh stood there watching, fascinated, as she rubbed her arms and legs to dry them, then tried to sop up as much water from the beaded dress as she possibly could. It was a losing battle.

"You could take it off," he offered helpfully.

"Yes, I could," she reflected aloud.

And damned if she didn't!

Right then. Right there.

Well, actually it took a few moments for her to get the dress off. Palm-dampening, mouth-parching, body-hardening moments as far as Hugh was concerned. Soaking-wet and clingy beaded dresses were obviously not easy to shed.

But as he stood there gaping, the crazy woman peeled the silvery straps of her beaded dress right down her arms and wriggled and shimmied and squirmed until the dress pooled at her feet and she was wearing a strapless bra and a pair of itsy-bitsy teeny-weeny bikini panties and nothing more.

Hugh's mouth went dry. His body got hot. He gaped, then tried to speak, but all he could manage was a croak like a frog's. Abruptly he shut his mouth.

The woman didn't seem to notice. She gave a huge sigh as she stepped neatly out of the pool of dress. "Thank God. You have no idea how heavy a wet beaded dress is."

No, he didn't. And if he tried to think about it, his mind whirled. All the blood that ordinarily made his brain function was far too busy elsewhere.

Without thinking, he sat down. Belle came and put her head on his knee, but her gaze was still on the crazy woman.

So was Hugh's.

"If we're going to be polite," the woman told him firmly, "you shouldn't stare. My father always told me it wasn't polite to stare."

Hugh swallowed, but he didn't stop staring. The ability to move his eyes was beyond him. His brain was still in neutral. Certain parts of his body, however, were on high alert.

"Huh?" he managed to croak at last, his gaze still impolitely roving over her slim but decidedly curvy form.

"What?" he said, aware that she had spoken yet unable to find the sense in her words.

"Whoa," he murmured as his brain finally engaged and he managed to both avert his gaze and shut his mouth at the same time. Major accomplishment. While his blood was otherwise occupied, the beer seemed to have gone to his head.

Now he tipped his head back and took a couple of deep, desperate breaths.

"Can I use this?" the crazy woman asked.

Her words made him jerk his head up, and he saw her holding up the quilt that Belle normally slept on. Belle was wagging her tail and grinning, apparently quite willing to share.

"Do you have to?"

He wasn't thinking, of course. He was just saying what came into his head. And what came into his head was how much he was enjoying the sight of all that lovely female flesh. And he was loath to lose sight of it, even when she gave him a seriously disdainful look.

"Then perhaps you could lend me your shirt." She looked at it pointedly. "Please," she added with more than a hint of irony.

He could. But leaving it flapping over his baggy shorts, thus hiding the evidence of his unfortunate arousal was probably a better idea.

"Use the quilt," he said gruffly.

She blinked, taken aback. But when he didn't change his mind, she shrugged and wrapped it around her shoulders, then clutched it over her middle, giving the impression that she had turned into an overstuffed chair.

Or she would have if Hugh hadn't had a good imagination and an even better memory. He knew damned well what was under the padding. He could still see it all in his mind's eye.

He was definitely glad he'd kept his shirt.

"So," he said, determined to focus on her less appealing characteristics, "tell me about this proactive jump of yours."

She glanced over her shoulder toward where the running

lights of the yacht were still barely visible. "Could we, um, just get moving first?"

"Catch up with them, you mean?" Hugh said doubtfully. It would be a hell of a ride in the dark.

"No!" The word burst out from her, surprising him. Then she gave herself a little shake. "I mean, no, thank you," she said with extreme politeness.

But even spoken with politeness, the words were still surprising. Hugh cocked his head and lifted a brow. "No, you don't want to catch up with the boat?"

"No!" Pause. Moderation. "I don't. In fact, I would very much like to head in the other direction."

"I'm not going in the other direction."

"Where are you going, then?" She looked suddenly apprehensive.

He jerked his head toward the lights of Pelican Cay. "There."

She turned to see where he'd indicated, and her apprehension faded a bit. She nodded her head. "That'll be fine," she said, glancing back at the lights of the yacht, then added, "Just let's go, okay?"

Interesting. And odd how she could swim in shark-infested waters with complete aplomb and then freak out when she was perfectly safe. Unless she wasn't perfectly safe.

"Did you steal something?" Hugh demanded, gaze narrowing.

"Steal something?" She looked shocked. "Whatever for?"

"How the hell should I know? You *jumped* off a bloody boat. Why the hell else would you run away?"

"I'm *not* running away!"

"Oh, right. I forgot. You were just proactively jumping into shark-infested waters miles from shore." He kept his tone conversational. It was easy enough to call her a liar with his eyes.

For an instant her gaze slid away, but then she brought

it back and met his squarely and Captain Ahab was back. "I needed to leave. That's all."

"Uh-huh."

"Look, will you just go?" she said. "I'll tell you. I promise. I haven't done anything wrong. I just need some space and a little time." She wasn't quite begging, but there was a definite urgency in her tone. She met his gaze steadily. "Please."

There was, even now, a sense of self-possession about her. As edgy as she was, it was a polite *please* not a frantic *please*.

Cripes, maybe it *had* been a proactive jump.

He nodded and moved to start the engine. She stepped out of his way. He got it going but didn't let out the throttle.

"What are you waiting for?" she demanded.

"You."

She looked blank.

"Can't go too fast," he explained. "I won't be able to hear you when you tell me why you jumped. And it better be good," he warned her, "to make up for my record catch that got away."

"I DON'T believe it," the scruffy fisherman said flatly when Sydney told him what had prompted her to jump overboard.

She glared at him. Who gave him the right to pass judgment, for heaven's sake? "Well, believe it or not, it's true."

"Let me get this straight. You jumped off a yacht in the middle of nowhere so you wouldn't have to get married?" He all but rolled his eyes as he repeated the gist of what she'd said.

Her jaw tightened. "More or less."

He rolled his eyes, then cocked his head and fixed his gaze on her. "Are you too young to remember the phrase Just Say No?"

"That was to say no to drugs."

"It is possible," the grubby fisherman pointed out, "to say no to other things."

"Like baths and clean clothes?" she said sweetly, her gaze raking him.

He had at least a couple of days' growth of beard on his face and he wore a pair of faded jean cutoffs and an equally faded short-sleeved shirt covered with outrageous cartoon flamingos and palm trees.

His dark brows drew down. "I'm clean," he protested. "I took a swim this afternoon."

"A swim?"

"Water's water. Don't change the subject. Why didn't you just say no? No, thank you," he corrected with a grin.

"Because," she told him haughtily, "it wouldn't have been efficacious." She doubted he even knew what the word meant.

He repeated it. "Efficacious. What's that when it's at home?"

"Appropriate. Though I doubt you know what that means, either."

"Me?" His brows went clear up into the fringe of hair that flopped over his forehead. "*I* don't know what's appropriate? Who jumped into the ocean miles from shore?"

She felt her face grow hot, but she refused to acknowledge the foolishness, even though now her knees were feeling like jelly. "It worked. They didn't see me. No one saw me."

"And that makes it appropriate?" He was almost shouting at her. "You're a flaming idiot, you know that? If I hadn't fished you out, you'd have drowned. Or been eaten by a shark."

"I saw your boat."

He stared at her as if she'd just escaped from Bedlam. "You saw my boat? A quarter of a bloody mile away?" He made it sound like rank idiocy. To him it obviously was. To her, at the time, it had been completely sensible and absolutely necessary.

There had been no other way.

She certainly couldn't call Roland Carruthers, her father's CEO, a liar! Not in front of the entire group of management and investors he'd brought together on the yacht to celebrate the acquisition of Butler Instruments by St. John Electronics.

And Roland had known it, damn him. That was why he hadn't said a word to her beforehand, but had simply stepped up to the microphone and announced their impending marriage.

Tonight, he'd said in his charming, dark whiskey voice, they were in for a delightful surprise. Everyone was going to get a living example of how much of a real family St. John Electronics was because they were all going to be witnesses at his shipboard marriage to Simon St. John's only daughter, Margaret Sydney St. John.

Her!

He had taken marriage—*her* marriage—and turned it into a business deal.

And then he'd had the temerity to meet her gaze and smile at her! As if she would approve!

Sydney had gone cold. And white. Stunned and speechless.

Which is probably exactly what he'd been counting on. And when she finally got her voice back, as he came over and put his arm around her shoulders and gave her a squeeze, she still couldn't say what she was thinking.

Because she knew better. Simon St. John had taught her well. The company always came first.

So there was no chance that Syd would undermine her father's firm or his representatives in public. She always did what was "best for the company." Corporate from her head to her toes, Syd would never gainsay his claim.

And Roland knew that. He'd played upon it, had counted on her agreement and on her going through with it because their marriage would be in the best interests of St. John Electronics.

But even though she might believe that, she couldn't do it.

Not like this.

His announcement had shocked her to her core. Only years of social conditioning had prevented her from showing it on her face. But whether she was more shocked by his announcement or by her own reaction to it was something she was going to have to think about.

If he'd *asked* her to marry him, if he'd wooed her, charmed her, pretended to love her, Syd had the sneaking suspicion she might have said yes.

But he hadn't. He'd presumed and simply expected her to go along with it—for the good of the company. Not because he loved her. Roland had never ever pretended to love her. They were business associates.

And yet he would have married her!

If she had been willing, Syd realized, she'd be Mrs. Roland Carruthers right now. No, she corrected herself, Roland would have been Mr. St. John Electronics.

Because it was all about business. Nothing else.

Yet if he had pretended—Syd shuddered to think about how close she might have come to agreeing, if he'd gone about it in a less manipulative fashion—she might have done it.

Thank God Roland dared to assume! Now she knew there was a line across which she wouldn't go.

No matter how good it would be for St. John Electronics, no matter how happy their marriage would make her father, she would not marry for the company.

She would only marry for love.

But she couldn't have said that in front of the guests!

She'd tried talking him out of it as he'd escorted her below to change into the silvery beaded dress. "This is crazy, Roland," she'd said. "You've had too much sun."

"On the contrary," he'd assured her, "it's exactly right. For everyone." He'd turned a deaf ear to all her objections. "You know it's for the best, Margaret." He always called her Margaret because her father did. "Don't act missish, my dear," he'd said, steering her toward her stateroom. "It's not like you."

No. It wasn't. But neither was just mindlessly doing what she was bullied into. And so she had shut the stateroom door on him.

"Hurry and change, Margaret," he'd said. "Everyone is waiting."

"I am not marrying you, Roland," she'd said through the door.

"Oh, Margaret, for goodness' sake," he'd said with irritating good humor. "Stop fussing and get a move on. I'll be on deck waiting for my bride."

He'd had a long wait.

Syd had changed into the party dress so she could give the impression of cooperating if anyone saw her, then she'd gone back out and along the passage to the stern. She'd climbed the ladder to the deck, then stayed out of sight until no one was looking.

And she'd jumped.

"I'm a strong swimmer," she told her sceptical rescuer firmly now. "I knew I could make it. And it was better than causing a fuss."

"Getting eaten by a shark wouldn't have caused a fuss?" He sounded furious. She didn't understand why. *He* wasn't the one who would have been fish food. But he was cracking his knuckles furiously and giving a sharp shake of his head.

"I didn't think there were any fish around," she said lamely.

His eyes flashed. "This is the ocean, sweetheart! Why the hell wouldn't there be any fish?"

"You weren't catching any," she pointed out.

He made a strangled sound, yanked off his ugly faded baseball cap and shoved his hand through shaggy dark hair that could have used cutting. "How could I catch any damn fish," he demanded, "with you kicking and floundering around out there? You were scaring them all away!"

"Even the sharks," she added.

The glower was mutual this time. And who knew how long it would have lasted if his dog hadn't nudged her way between them. Obviously a peacemaker. The dog—a border collie, Syd thought—grinned at her, looking much more reputable and a good deal friendlier than the fisherman.

Venturing a hand out to scratch the dog's ears, Syd asked, "What's her name?"

For a minute she didn't think he was going to tell her. He pressed his lips together, then shrugged. "Belle."

The dog wagged her tail at the sound of her name.

"Hello, Belle," Syd crooned, rubbing the soft ears and getting rewarded with a lick of her hands. "You're beautiful. I'm Syd."

"*Sid?*" Belle's owner echoed in disbelief.

"Syd with a *Y*. Sydney." She hesitated, too, then told him her full name, "Margaret Sydney St. John," and waited for the jolt of recognition.

He looked at her with no recognition at all. No awareness that he was talking to the woman whose father had invented one of the most important telecommunications networks in the world, a woman whose name had been all over the Bahamian papers in recent days as she and Roland Carruthers had been negotiating a buyout of a high-profile Bahamian firm. No clue that, according to people in the know, he was talking to one of the most eligible women in America.

He just looked blank, then reluctantly stuck out a fishy-smelling hand and said, "Hugh McGillivray."

McGillivray. It figured.

He had that raw Scottish warrior look to him. Syd could imagine him with his face painted blue. She wondered how he'd look in a kilt and was surprised at the direction of her thoughts.

Abruptly she jerked them back to the moment and, reluctantly, took his offered hand. It was every bit as unnerving as she'd imagined it would be.

Used to shaking the soft hands of boardroom execs, she felt the difference immediately. Hugh McGillivray's palm was hard and rough. There was a ragged bloody scratch on the back of his hand.

"Shark bite?" she asked.

His gaze narrowed. A corner of his mouth twitched. But then he shook his head solemnly. "Barracuda."

She jerked and blinked in surprise, then swallowed hastily. "Really?"

Hugh McGillivray gave her an unholy grin. "Gotcha."

HE DIDN'T believe a word of it.

Nobody jumped overboard to avoid getting married. It was preposterous. Ridiculous. Out of the question.

But it was her story and she'd stuck to it. Or at least she had so far.

Crazy woman.

Hugh shot her a glance now as he slowed the boat and headed it into Pelican Cay's small harbor. Once she'd told him her amazing tale, he'd revved the engine and headed for the island, full speed ahead. Still, it had taken close to half an hour to get there, and the sun had gone down completely now.

In the darkness reflections streamed across the water from the row of street lamps along the quay and from the houses that fronted the harbor. The small houses that climbed the low hill of Pelican Town looked almost like dolls' houses, tidy and laid-back and welcoming all at once.

Home. Hugh smiled as he always did at the sight, though he doubted it would impress Miss Margaret Sydney St. John. Why ever she did or didn't jump off the boat, she'd clearly been on it. And that—and the way she looked down her lovely nose at him—told him that she was from a higher rung on the social ladder than him and most of the people who lived in Pelican Town or who made their living on the fishing boats bobbing in the harbor tonight.

Folks like them didn't name their girls Sydney for one

thing. Hugh snorted, thinking about it. Hell of a stupid name for a girl. He supposed her old man had been counting on a son.

Probably she was a "junior," he thought with a wry grin. From what she'd said he gathered that her old man was married to his company and thought his daughter was merely an extension of it.

Not that she'd been complaining. God, no.

She had actually defended the old man and St. John Electronics fervently when he'd asked her why the hell she would care if she embarrassed its CEO by telling him hell no she wasn't going to marry him.

"I couldn't do that!" she'd protested. "It would have made the company look bad if Roland and I were at odds. Besides, it would upset my father."

"You don't think maybe hearing his daughter had been eaten by a shark would have upset him?" Hugh had demanded.

He was almost sorry he'd been so blunt when she'd gone white in the moonlight. It was, he realized, the first time she really seemed to consider the concrete implications of what she'd done.

But even then she'd given herself a little shake.

"I wasn't eaten," she'd reminded him almost defiantly.

But her tone didn't sound quite as firm as it had. And she'd clutched the quilt around her even more tightly and determinedly looked away.

Hugh had left her to it. He'd kicked up the speed and focused on the island, only glancing her way occasionally and scowling as she looped an arm companionably over Belle and drew his dog inside the quilt with her.

Belle was still there now, snuggled in. Hugh shut his eyes and tried not to think about it.

He was having way too strong a reaction to Margaret Sydney St. John. It disconcerted him. The only woman who'd inspired anything like it had been Carin—for all the good that had done him. He had no interest in having reactions like that ever again—and certainly not about a crazy woman!

It wasn't really her *per se,* he assured himself, gorgeous though she was. It was just the lack of any other woman in his life. In his bed.

Plagued as he had been every waking moment this summer by the determined attentions of the sweet marriageable Lisa, he'd found other women tended to give him a wide berth.

"You have a girlfriend," they always explained when they turned him down for dates.

"She's *not* my girlfriend!" Hugh had claimed over and over.

But the protest fell on deaf ears. And on Lisa's ears. And Lisa ignored them.

"Well, if I'm not your girlfriend, who is?" Lisa had asked confidently.

"I don't have a girlfriend!" he'd protested.

Too much.

Women! Hugh despaired of them. They were all crazy as loons.

At least this one—Miss Margaret Sydney St. John— would be out of his life damn quick.

As soon as he got her to shore, he'd take her to the Moonstone, his brother Lachlan's inn, where she could spend the night. From there she could call Daddy. In the morning her old man could come rescue her, and she'd be gone within the day.

Hugh would never see her again and that would be fine with him.

He was still a little nettled that she hadn't been a big fish.

She'd jerked his line exactly like a big fish, he thought irritably. Lachlan was going to laugh his head off when he heard that Hugh had caught a woman.

Behind him the woman he'd caught drew in a sharp

breath. He looked around. "What's the matter now?" he asked gruffly.

"Nothing's the matter. It's—" she waved her hand toward the harbor and the town "—so beautiful. That's all. It's like paradise." She beamed at him.

Hugh knew what she meant. He felt exactly the same way. But he scowled because he didn't like the way her approval and her smile had slipped under his defenses. He rubbed a hand against the back of his neck.

"I like it," he admitted. He spent a moment savoring it again before he continued, "But it's not exactly ritzy. There are a few inns and resorts on the windward side of the island. One pretty posh one on the north end. The Mirabelle. My brother owns it. I'll take you there for the night."

"No!" Her rejection was a yelp.

Hugh frowned. "What do you mean, no?"

"Sorry. I just mean, I don't want to go there."

"You've never even seen it! It's beautiful. A class place. Maybe not five-star like I'm sure you're accustomed to…" he drawled, irritated now.

"I don't care how many stars it does or doesn't have. I don't want to go to an inn or a resort. I want to be… incognito."

His mouth quirked. "Incognito, huh?" He doubted if Sydney St. John had ever said the word *incognito* before, much less applied it to herself. Even in her current padded-blanket guise with salt-encrusted hair clumped and straggly, she was a shockingly beautiful—and memorable—woman.

"Yeah," he said, looking her slowly up and down. "I can see you being incognito. Sure. Right."

She tossed her head. "I can be. I need to be!" she said fiercely. "I have to think about what to do, how to handle things."

"You could already have handled things," Hugh felt obliged to point out, "if you'd just said no in the first place."

She gave him an impatient look. "I already told you, I couldn't. It would have messed up everything."

He couldn't see that, but obviously he wasn't as crazy as she was. Nor was he a woman. He figured you'd have to be one or the other to have it make sense to you. "Well, fine. Whatever. Then there's the Moonstone. It's pretty cool. An old Victorian place."

"No inns."

He rolled his eyes. "Then stay at a B&B. We've got at least half a dozen of those."

"Too public. He'd check."

"So what are you planning to do? Sleep on the beach?" he asked sarcastically.

She missed the sarcasm. "I'd be far too noticeable if I did that." She cast about and spied the sleeping bag beneath the bow. "I'll sleep here," she said brightly.

"The hell you will!"

He could just see that—the fishermen of Pelican Cay grumbling and bumbling their way down to their boats in the morning and getting an eyeful of Sydney St. John crawling out of his sleeping bag.

She'd shock the socks off the entire fleet! And then what would she do? Amble down the dock to use the facilities at the Customs house dressed in nothing but Belle's quilt? Or worse, *without* Belle's quilt!

Hugh shook his head vehemently, cutting the engine off as they drifted toward the dock. "Not on your life. Uh-uh. No way. Don't even think it."

But obviously she was. "I wouldn't hurt anything. I'd clean up after myself." She looked around the boat. "After you," she amended, wrinkling her nose. "This boat could use a good scrubbing."

"It's a boat, for God's sake, not a floor," he protested. They bumped against the rubber-tire-edged dock.

"Even so, a little soap and water wouldn't hurt it," she informed him primly.

"No." He grabbed the stern line and wrapped it around

the cleat on the dock, then jumped out to do the same with the bow.

The crazy woman followed him, letting Belle out of the quilt and giving Hugh tantalizing glimpses of bare flesh. "Don't be so negative, McGillivray," she bargained. "Just one night. Or two. I'll scrub the decks for you. Slap on some paint. I like being useful."

"No. You'd give the fishermen heart attacks." He jumped back into the boat and brushed past her, reaching for the cooler.

"I could stay hidden until they left."

"No."

"Then how about if I stay with you?"

"Me?" Hugh blanched and jerked around to glare at her. "You don't want to stay with me."

"I certainly don't," she agreed readily. "But I need somewhere that Roland won't find me."

"Not my place. I live in a shack."

Which wasn't quite true. His place was small, granted, but it wasn't falling down. It overlooked the beach on the windward side of the island. It was old and comfortable. Perfect for him—and far too small for entertaining the likes of Sydney St. John.

"A shack, huh? Why am I not surprised?" she murmured.

He rose to the bait. "By your standards," he clarified, "it would be a shack. By mine it's just right."

"I'm sure it is. And for me it will be, too—for a short time. Just until I get my head together, McGillivray. Just until I figure out a plan of action. And give Roland pause for thought. I won't be any trouble," she promised.

And if he believed that, next thing you knew she'd be selling him a bridge from Nassau to Miami.

"There is no room," Hugh said firmly. "It's just a little beach house. Not your style."

"How do you know my style?"

"I know women."

"Oh, really?"

The doubt that dripped from her words infuriated him. He did know women. They'd been coming on to him since he was fourteen years old. And generally speaking they liked what they saw. It was only Sydney St. John who looked at him as if she'd found him on the sole of her shoe.

"Like I said," he told her gruffly, "I'm not your style."

"I can stand anything for a few days," she informed him.

"Well, I can't. And there is nothing you can say that will—" He broke off at the sound of a shrill, happy voice calling his name from the end of the quay. He gritted his teeth and shut his eyes. "Damn it to hell."

Sydney St. John looked at him, startled. "What?"

"Nothing." He finished tossing the last of the gear onto the dock, grabbed his bag with one hand and took Syd's arm none too gently with the other. Then he turned toward the woman approaching them and managed a casual and determinedly indifferent, "Hey, there, Lisa. How you doing?"

Lisa flashed him her beautiful, dimpled smile even as she looked curiously at the woman he held firmly at his side. "I'm all right," she said, her voice a little hesitant for once. "But I was a little lonely. I thought you'd get back sooner than this."

"I told you I had, um…business," Hugh said vaguely.

"Business?" The smile wavered as Lisa looked at Syd. "Of course," she said, slotting Syd into that role. "I didn't realize you were bringing a client back with you." She gave Syd a polite smile, then turned back to Hugh. "I made conch chowder this evening. I figured I'd bring it over when you got back."

He shook his head. "Thanks, Lisa. I appreciate the thought. But we're fine."

Lisa's smile faltered as he had hoped it would. "We?" Perplexed, she looked from Hugh to the woman standing beside him, the woman whose wrist he had a death grip on.

"We," Hugh confirmed. He let go of her wrist long enough to loop an arm over her shoulders. "This is Syd—" he began, but Sydney cut him off before he got to her last name.

"I'm very pleased to meet you," she said smoothly and offered Lisa a hand.

Lisa looked at it warily, but finally shook it, giving the quilt—and the bits of bare Sydney she could see—an assessing look. "You, too, um, Syd," she said doubtfully even as she managed to paste the smile back on. "I'm Lisa. Are you staying at the Mirabelle? Or the Moonstone?"

"No," Hugh said before Sydney St. John could say anything at all. "She's staying with me."

If she was astonished at his sudden about-face, at least Syd didn't say a word. It was what she wanted, after all. She'd practically begged him to let her stay with him, hadn't she?

So he was doing them both a favor.

Roland Wheeler Dealer would get a few days of worrying about whether he'd drowned the boss's daughter, and Hugh would have a beautiful sexy woman living in his house.

If that didn't convince Lisa once and for all that he was not interested in her, he didn't know what would.

Yes, of course Sydney St. John was a little bit whacko and more than a little bit gorgeous. And yes, all his hormones had sat up and taken note.

So what? He could handle it.

It was one night. Maybe two. At the most, three.

How bad could it possibly be?

CHAPTER TWO

"DON'T go using *me* to make your girlfriend jealous!" Syd protested as McGillivray, his arm still wrapping her shoulders like a vise, hustled her down the dock toward the quay. Over her shoulder she could see Lisa staring after them, lower lip trembling.

"She's *not* my girlfriend!"

"Then why is she cooking you conch chowder and meeting your boat?"

"Because she wants to be my girlfriend," McGillivray said through gritted teeth, sounding beleaguered as he dragged her along.

She clutched at the quilt, nearly tripping, as she hurried to keep up. "Really? Your girlfriend? Why? She looks far too sensible to me!"

"I wish," McGillivray muttered. "And God knows why," he added. "I sure don't."

They reached a rusty, topless Jeep parked at the foot of the dock, and he tossed his gear into the back, then jerked open the door for her. "Come on. Get in. We don't have all day."

"Oh?" It was interesting to see how the girl, Lisa, had spooked McGillivray. He didn't look the sort to be afraid of women. Tucking the quilt up, Syd climbed into the Jeep. "What's the problem, then? Does she want to save you from yourself?"

He barely let her get her feet in before he banged the door shut behind her. "That's what my sister says." He gave a short sharp whistle and slapped the wheel. "Come on, Belle! Move it."

Belle took a leap and landed in the back, on top of McGillivray's bag, some pots and pans, a few unidentified tools, a couple of grease-streaked T-shirts and some paper bags that looked as if they had once contained take-out meals. K-rations, Syd thought. And they'd probably been there since World War II. General Patton would have been right at home. "What a mess."

Her opinion of his Jeep and its contents didn't seem to matter to McGillivray. He ignored her and ruffled the dog's fur. Then he turned and loped back up the dock. He stopped to have a brief conversation with Lisa as he piled into her arms a bunch of the stuff he'd taken from the boat and put on the dock. Then he hoisted the cooler into his own arms, and they walked back to the Jeep together.

Syd stared. If Lisa wasn't his girlfriend, what was she? His packhorse?

"Thanks," Hugh said cheerfully to Lisa when they got there. "Just toss all that stuff in the back with Belle."

Lisa did. And when she did, Syd noted that the "stuff" included her beaded dress. Lisa had obviously noticed it, too. She swallowed hard, but then smiled again with clear determination.

McGillivray didn't appear to notice. He was whistling as he stowed the cooler in the back of the Jeep. "Thanks a lot," he said breezily, then jumped into the Jeep, flicked on the key already stuck in the ignition. "You're a pal, Lise."

Lisa looked stricken.

McGillivray just stomped the gas pedal, and they shot off up the street.

"You hurt her feelings!" Syd remonstrated as they bounced along.

McGillivray shrugged and hit another pothole. The narrow street was paved but there were more potholes than tarmac as it climbed the hill straight up from the dock. On both sides she saw wooden and stucco houses and shops. Most of the people walking about called out a greeting to Hugh, who waved carelessly back as they bounced up the hill.

Most of the houses they passed had small front gardens or none at all. Some had high walls that butted right against the street. Others had broad overhung porches. All of them, as far as Syd could tell in the minimal light from the few scattered street lamps, looked to be of the same vintage as the Jeep or a hundred or so years older. All of them were in better repair than the street itself.

"Hang on," McGillivray suggested as he took a hard right and she nearly bounced out. "I've lost a few passengers who haven't."

Slowly, casually—his earlier "gotcha" still ringing in her ears—Syd reached out to take hold of the bar at the side of the windshield. Just then the Jeep hit a particularly wide and deep pothole, and she scrabbled for a grip to save herself from lurching over the side.

She turned to glare at McGillivray.

"Warned you." He grinned.

A dozen or so potholes later, he took a sharp left past a broad open field, and then right onto a gravel track into the trees. Abruptly they left the small town behind and plunged into the blackness. Now the road seemed barely wider than the Jeep, and the vegetation rose up on both sides to meet above them. Even with the headlights' illumination, Syd couldn't make out a thing. Through the foliage Syd caught sight of occasional lights. Lamps in windows, she surmised as the Jeep slowed and McGillivray whipped it sharply first right, then left, then right again and all at once, a wall loomed in front of them. McGillivray braked, spraying dirt and gravel, then cut the engine.

"Home sweet home," he announced.

Syd breathed again. Once. Then Belle leaped out and McGillivray followed.

"Come on," he said to Syd. "And watch out for snakes."

"*Snakes?*" Dear God. Syd huddled deeper into the quilt. But even as she sat there she heard his footsteps disappearing around the side of the building. And in the silence there were rustlings in the shrubbery, the sound of branches cracking, slitherings—

"Wait! I'm coming!" She leaped out of the Jeep, hitched up the quilt and flew after him. Breathless, heart pounding, she rounded the corner of the house just as the porch light went on.

Correction: porch *lights*. A whole string of glowing pink flamingos interspersed with neon-green palm trees dangled along the edge of his roof.

"Why am I not surprised?" Syd muttered. "All you need now is a string of hula girls."

"Wrong islands," he said cheerfully from the doorway. "But I didn't let that stop me," he said as he flipped another switch and strings of hula girls lit up each of the porch columns.

Syd sputtered, but she couldn't help laughing. "What does your girlfriend think of these?"

"She's *not* my girlfriend!"

"Right." But if saying so would get a rise of out him, Syd didn't mind doing it. She was still smiling as she climbed the four shallow steps to the porch, which was as cluttered as the Jeep had been, scattered with swim fins, snorkles and fishing nets, assorted pots and pans, a dog bed, food and water dishes and myriad unidentifiable mechanical objects.

A net hammock was strung across one end of the porch, and a long slatted-wood porch swing swayed at the other. Behind the latter were tucked a surfboard and a boogie board. Above it a disembodied wet suit swung lazily from a clothes hanger on a plant hook. The plant that it might have displaced was balanced precariously on the porch railing.

He was right. It wasn't close to the five-star hotel she had left behind on Nassau. On the other hand, no one was announcing her betrothal as if it were on the dinner menu here.

And so far she hadn't seen any snakes.

"How lovely," she said brightly, stepping over a pan.

McGillivray gave her a doubtful look. But Syd met it with a cheerful, determined one of her own. And she must have been convincing because he said gruffly, "C'mon. Don't just stand there. You'll want a shower. I'll find you some clothes."

The chaos extended into the kitchen, where newspapers and magazines were scattered amid pots and pans. There were some engine parts on one chair and a pile of laundry on another. Yet another pile was on the floor. The sink, of course, held dirty dishes.

"I thought hurricane season was in the autumn," Syd remarked.

"Bothers you, do something about it." McGillivray was busy rummaging through one of the clothes heaps. The clean one, Syd hoped when he pulled out a navy T-shirt and a pair of shorts, surveyed the pile, hesitated, then turned and thrust them at her. "You want a pair of boxers?"

She blinked. "What?"

"I said, do you want a pair of boxers? You're, er—" he gestured down below her waist but couldn't seem to say the word "—wet," he finally managed, scowling.

Was that a tinge of red creeping up his neck and touching the tips of his ears?

His face was definitely red. Talking about women's underwear embarrassed Hugh McGillivray?

Who'd have thought it? "That would be nice. Thank you," Syd said politely, smothering a smile.

He gave her another long, baleful look before reaching back into the pile and snagging a pair of pale-blue boxer shorts to toss in her direction. "You can borrow some clothes from my sister tomorrow if you want. Not that Mol has any girls' clothes, either,'' he added with a grimace. ''Or you can go shopping. Shower's this way.'' He turned abruptly and headed toward the back of the house.

Syd clutched the clothes, hiked up her quilt and followed him. To the left she saw what appeared to be a small living room, but McGillivray went straight back through a bedroom toward a door that led to a tiny bathroom. At least he had indoor plumbing. She'd begun to worry.

He also had one clean towel. At least she presumed it was, because he got it out of the cupboard. He turned on the shower taps. ''Let the water run. It'll get hot eventually. Don't use it all up.''

''I won't,'' she assured him.

But he was already on his way out the door. ''Watch out for spiders.''

''*Spiders?*'' She looked around wildly.

McGillivray grinned wickedly over his shoulder. ''Gotcha,'' he mouthed.

She wanted to kill him.

''A woman who isn't afraid of sharks shouldn't let a little spider or two bother her,'' he said. ''I'll fix us something to eat.'' The door banged shut behind him.

There were no spiders. There were no snakes. She was alone. And suddenly every bit of the adrenaline that had been fueling her since Roland's astonishing announcement vanished.

Her breath came in quick thready gasps. Her heart beat in a crazy staccato rhythm. Her vision darkened, and the room seemed to spin.

''Oh, help!'' She groped for something to hang on to and grabbed the towel rack—right off the wall.

The door burst open.

''For God's sake!'' McGillivray kicked the towel rack aside and crouched beside her on the floor. ''What the hell happened?''

''N-nothing. I…n-nothing.'' She tried to get up, but found herself shoved down again and held fast.

"Did you faint?"

"Of course not!" But her brain was still spinning and her legs felt like mush. Even so, she squirmed against his hold.

"Stay still," McGillivray commanded and thrust her head unceremoniously between her knees. "Take deep breaths—and don't faint again!"

"I *didn't faint!*" she said again for all the good it did her.

As if it were a matter of choice, anyway, she thought grimly, sucking in oxygen, doing her best not to make a liar out of herself, while a firm hand pressed against the back of her neck.

"Breathe, damn it."

"I'm trying—" gulp, gulp "—to."

"Then stop talking. Breathe deeper. Big breaths."

God, he was bossy! "I'm all right," she protested. "I just…tripped."

"Yeah, right. Breathe."

She did. And the blood thrummed in her ears and her heart slammed against the wall of her chest. But gradually her heart slowed, her vision returned. McGillivray's callused hand, though, held her head firmly down.

She shifted. "I'm all right now," she insisted, and pushed back against his hand.

He eased the pressure a bit. "Take it easy." He watched her warily as she straightened up, as if expecting her to go headfirst onto the floor again.

Determined not to, she took another deep breath and sat up straight. The quilt fell away from her shoulders.

McGillivray's breath hissed through his teeth. Reaching over, he jerked the quilt back up and wrapped it tightly around her again.

Surprised, Syd looked up at him.

He glared back at her. "What?"

"Nothing. I just…you seem…" She was babbling, but

she couldn't help it. "I didn't think—" But it did make sense of things.

"You didn't think what?" he demanded.

"That you were gay."

"What?" He jerked as if she'd shot him. "What the hell do you mean, I'm gay?" McGillivray's voice was a roar.

"Well, you keep covering me up!" Syd shouted back at him. "As if the sight offends you! I know I'm no raving beauty—" God knew Roland had been quite capable of resisting her "—but I'm passably attractive. At least, no one else has ever been at such pains not to have to look at me."

He snorted and scrambled to his feet, as if putting as much distance between them as he could. "And that makes me gay?"

"I just thought... You said Lisa wasn't your girlfriend. You were very...adamant about it. And you said your sister thought she was trying to, um, save you from yourself."

It all made sense as far as Syd could see. "I don't mind if you are," she told him.

"Is that supposed to be comforting?"

"Well, I—"

He straightened up, wincing a little as he did so, then glowered down at her. "Do I look like I'm gay, sweetheart?" he drawled.

From her vantage point, at the level of his hairy, tanned knees, Syd looked slowly up—and came to the very obvious evidence that he was not.

"Oh," she said in a very small voice.

McGillivray looked somewhere between pained and gratified at her realization. "Exactly," he muttered.

Syd knew her face was burning. "Um...sorry. Is there...anything I can do?"

McGillivray goggled at her. "Are you for real?"

God, she might go up in flames! "I didn't mean *that!*" she protested. "I just—never mind!" Obviously, she wasn't good at this sort of thing.

"I'll live," McGillivray said dryly in the face of her
confusion. Then he reached out a hand. "Here. Can you
stand on your own two feet?"

"Yes, of course." She would have declined his hand
altogether but she was afraid she might fall over if she did.
But somehow, touching him, knowing the effect she'd had
on him, made her let go the second she was upright. "I'm
all right," she assured him. "Really. I just got a bit light-
headed for a moment. I *didn't* faint!" she added when she
saw the gleam in his eyes.

"Whatever you say," he replied gravely, but the gleam
was still there.

And something else.

Attraction? Certainly it was something electric. Awareness seemed to sizzle between them for just a moment.

Abruptly, McGillivray looked away. His jaw tightened,
and he wiped his hands down the sides of his shorts and
turned toward the door.

"Hurry up," he told her, his voice raspy. "I'm burning
the bacon."

The door banged shut behind him, and Syd was left in
the same bathroom she'd been in moments before.

But something had changed. Something was different.
There was an electricity lingering in the air. Syd was used
to electricity. She felt it whenever she was in the midst of
closing a business deal, when things were coming together,
when an energy seemed to take over of its own accord.

It felt like that now.

And there was no business deal. No business at all.

Just awareness. Man-woman awareness. McGillivray had
wanted her. Physically.

Intellectually, of course, Syd knew all about that sort of
thing. Men—heterosexual ones—lusted after women. But,
generally speaking, men had never really lusted after *her*.

They had mostly been interested in her as her father's
daughter. Roland certainly hadn't given her cause for be-
lieving that his interest in marrying her had anything to do

with her innate attractiveness. He had been going to marry her because it was good for business.

He'd never even pretended otherwise.

How mortifying was that?

Pretty mortifying. But it would have been even more so if McGillivray hadn't so clearly felt otherwise.

She felt suddenly, exquisitely, aware of her own nakedness.

She'd stripped her dress off in the boat without even thinking, without expecting a reaction at all. She'd never even considered he might react. Roland had been impervious to her charms. Why should she have expected anyone else to succumb?

Not that McGillivray had succumbed, she reminded herself, as she stepped beneath the shower spray. But he had been interested. Physically responsive.

The knowledge made her smile. It made her feel alive. It made her feel desirable in her own right—as a woman—and not just as an asset to the St. John Electronics company.

She tipped some of McGillivray's shampoo into her hands and began rubbing it into her hair. It smelled of lime and the sea and something else she couldn't quite put a name to. But it was fresh and sharp, and she liked it more than she liked the flowery English-garden stuff she was accustomed to.

It was a new beginning.

She liked the sound of that. She stuck her head under the showerhead and lathered up vigorously, washing Roland Carruthers right out of her hair. And St. John Electronics, too. Then she ducked her head beneath the shower and watched the lather disappear down the drain. In seconds it was gone.

She was clean, fresh, unencumbered.

And desirable.

An intriguing thought.

Syd turned off the water, toweled herself off and dressed in the clothes McGillivray had given her. Then, for luck, she dabbed a tiny bit of McGillivray's lime-scented after-shave on her pulse points—and began to plot the future.

THIS might have been a mistake—bringing Sydney St. John home with him.

The woman was a menace, Hugh thought, banging around the kitchen, trying not to think about the naked woman showering just beyond that closed bathroom door. She was ten times more tempting than Lisa Milligan had ever thought of being, and she didn't even seem to know it.

And because he had done his best to preserve her modesty, she'd thought he was gay!

He'd never felt less gay in his life!

He stood at the kitchen counter now, in theory chopping up onions for an omelette, but in fact he had his eyes shut while in his mind he could still see her as she'd shimmied out of that beaded dress on the boat. Judging from his re-actions, his body remembered the view even better than his mind did.

And the glimpse he'd got when that quilt had fallen away just moments ago hadn't helped cool his ardor. He didn't need any more views like that one, thank you very much—not unless she was going to follow it up with a little action.

Fat chance.

Wasn't going to happen.

He wasn't going to let it happen, because Sydney St. John—for all her clothes shedding and shimmying—was no different than Lisa Milligan. If she had been telling the truth about what had happened on the yacht—and she had to be, simply because her story was so ridiculous she couldn't possibly have made it up!—then she was obvi-ously an idealist. She'd refused to marry Roland What's-His-Name for business reasons. Ergo, she must have some romantic notion about marrying for love.

Nothing wrong with that.

Hugh believed in it himself. It was exactly what he had wanted with Carin.

But he couldn't have Carin, so he had learned to want something else. Fun. Games. A night's romp with no strings attached.

It didn't take a genius to see that Sydney St. John had more strings than a tennis racket. There would be no romping with her.

"Not gonna happen," he told Belle. "No sir. No way."

So when Sydney St. John waltzed into the kitchen fifteen minutes later, he was prepared.

Or he thought he was—until he caught a glimpse of her breasts bobbing beneath the soft cotton of his navy blue T-shirt and her endless legs below the hem of his boxer shorts. Then his firm commitment and his well-planned words dried right up.

"Well, that was refreshing," she said, beaming at him. "I feel so-o-o much better."

She looked better, too, if that were possible. She had her long hair tucked up inside a towel which made her look almost regal in a Queen Nefertiti sort of way—all neck and turban.

And breasts. And legs. No way could he forget the breasts and legs. Hugh swallowed hard.

"Glad to hear it," he managed, and was relieved that he didn't sound like a fourteen-year-old. Just to be sure, he cleared his throat before he went on. "Sit down. Dig in." He dumped an omelette on her plate, then gestured toward a plateful of toast and several bowls of leftovers from Lisa's earlier seduction efforts. "Then we need to get some things straight."

"Sure." Syd gave him a bright smile. Her breasts jiggled beneath his T-shirt as she sat down. Hugh looked away as she took a bite of omelette, then began heaping salad and coleslaw onto her plate.

"This is great! Did you cook all this? I can't cook a thing," she admitted cheerfully. She swallowed the omelette, then took a big bite of the coleslaw and closed her eyes blissfully. "God, it's good. I'm famished."

She dug in, plowing her way through the eggs, the toast, the bacon, the leftover slaw and salad and chicken wings Lisa had fixed. Hugh tried not to watch. She was just a woman eating, for heaven's sake. Nothing spectacular about that.

Except that she relished it so much, sighing happily, smacking her lips. Watching her attack a chicken wing was like watching that old movie *Tom Jones*. Except she was a damned sight sexier than whoever that woman had been playing opposite Albert Finney. And the sexual undercurrents weren't on the screen, they were in Hugh's head. He jumped up and paced around the room.

"Something the matter?" she asked, following him with her gaze.

"No!" The word came out more as a snap than as a word. "I'm just...making some coffee. Do you want some coffee?"

"That would be wonderful."

He made a pot of coffee. And while he was doing it, he got a grip. He remembered again all the things he needed to say to make sure they both got through the next day or so unscathed. And when it had finished dripping, he poured two mugs and carried them over to the table.

He set one in front of her and took one to the other side of the table where he sat down opposite her with slow deliberation, intending to make sure she understood how very serious he was.

She took the coffee gratefully, then started in on the chicken again.

Hugh averted his gaze. "Rule number one," he said.

She looked up, fork halfway to her mouth, which was shaped like an *O*. She blinked. "Rule what?"

He set his jaw. "We need some ground rules. So you don't get any mistaken ideas."

"So I don't..." Her voice trailed off. She put the forkful

of potato salad in her mouth, closed it again, then began to chew slowly as if she were chewing over his words as well as the food. All the while her very blue eyes never left his. He felt his blood pressure going up.

At last she swallowed. "Right," she said finally. "Ground rules." She set down her fork and folded her hands in her lap. "By all means."

There was something in her voice—sarcasm?—that made him narrow his gaze. She smiled at him.

He scowled at her. "I don't want you getting any ideas."

"Ideas?" By God, she looked as if butter wouldn't melt in her mouth. "About what?"

"About us," he bit out.

"*Us?*" Her eyes grew like saucers.

"Yes, us. You and me." He spelled it out. "On account of what happened before. In there." He jerked his head toward the bathroom.

Her brows lifted fractionally. "Oh. I see. When you demonstrated your heterosexuality, you mean?"

Her expression was perfectly bland, but Hugh knew when someone was having a go at him. His jaw clenched. He had to force himself to unlock it. "Call it whatever you want. The point is, don't get the idea that I'm interested, because I'm not!"

She smiled. "Could've fooled me," she said brightly, then picked up her fork again and took a big bite.

Hugh strangled his own fork to keep from strangling her neck. "I didn't agree to let you stay here to keep Lisa away only to have you thinking along the same lines!" he informed her flatly.

Sydney St. John's eyes bugged. "*That's* the idea you don't want me getting? You think I want to *marry* you? My God, I didn't even want to marry Roland, and he at least had a job to recommend him."

Now it was Hugh's turn to blink. She didn't think he had a job? Well, fine. Let her think what she wanted.

"Right," he said. "Wouldn't want to distract you from your headlong dash toward spinsterhood."

She sputtered into her coffee, then visibly pulled herself together and informed him haughtily, "Spinsterhood has a great deal to recommend it. More and more every minute," she told him, breasts heaving beneath the soft cotton of the T-shirt she wore.

Hugh cleared his throat again. "Glad to hear you think so," he said. "But just to make sure you remember it," he went on, refusing to be distracted, "I think a few rules would make things easier during the short time you're here." He came down hard on the word *short*.

Sydney shrugged negligently. "Frankly I'm pretty sick of rules," she told him. "I've followed the rules all my life, and look where it's got me."

He didn't want to look at where it had got her. He just wanted her gone. "Rule number one," he persisted. "You get your own clothes tomorrow."

The sooner she stopped wearing his, the saner and more sensible he would feel.

"If someone will extend me some credit," she said. "I don't want to give out my credit card number for a few days, or Roland will be able to find out where I am."

"I'll lend you some cash," Hugh promised. "Rule number two—"

"You don't look like a man who likes rules."

"I don't," Hugh said before he thought.

"Then why do we need them?" Syd asked.

Because I'd like to jump your bones, didn't seem like the best response. "I thought it would make you more comfortable," he said somewhat stiffly.

"Well, I'm not," she said, and set down her coffee with a thump. "I'm finished with rules. I've made up my mind. I'm done with doing what I'm supposed to do." The Captain Ahab chin tilted again.

Seeing it actually made a corner of Hugh's mouth lift. She had guts, did Syd St. John, he'd give her that.

"Good for you," he said, nodding and thinking Roland Carruthers deserved a little payback.

Syd beamed at him. "You think so? Great!" She leaned intently toward him across the table, her blue eyes alight. "I thought about it all the time I was taking a shower—about how I'd got into this mess. I thought about what happened tonight on the yacht and everything that led up to it. I thought about Roland and about my father. About his expectations—and mine. About where I've been and where I'm going." She straightened up and gave a firm little jerk of her head. "And I've decided it's going to be different from here on out. Completely different."

Hugh saw the way she was looking at him for approval, and nodded his head "Right. You show 'em."

"I will! I've spent twenty-seven years living by rules. My father's rules. My father's expectations. My fault, not his," she said quickly. "I know that. But the point is, following them didn't do any good. I tried to be the sweet malleable daughter he wanted, and I tried to be the take-over-the-business son he never had. And I was just a cog in the machine. I was never a person who mattered. So I'm done with it! From now on, I'm going to be me."

Hugh gave her a grin and a thumbs-up. "Good for you."

"First, though, I have to figure out who me is." She beamed at him.

"Good idea." He understood the concept. He'd discovered it himself when he'd come up against the Navy's rules and regs. There were things he'd loved about the Navy, but in the end, it wasn't him. "So, what are you going to do?" he asked her.

"I'm going to live a little!"

The way she said it, it didn't sound like a *little*. It sounded as if she intended to live a whole hell of a lot.

Hugh tipped back in his chair. "Which means what? Besides your not wanting any rules?"

"It means I'm going to stop putting St. John Electronics first. I'm going to stop trying to be the son my father never had. I'm going to stop doing what's expected of me and do what I want to do!'' She paused, then plunged on. ''First thing tomorrow, I'm going to get a job.''

He stared. ''What do you mean, you're going to get a job?''

''Well, I can't presume on your hospitality forever.''

''Amen to that,'' he muttered. ''But you can't get a job. You don't live here.''

''I think I might.''

''What!'' The feet of the chair hit the floor with a crash.

Sydney shrugged. ''Why not? I have talent. I have skills.''

''Oh, yes? Knowing which fork to use is a great talent. Can you arrange a charity luncheon with one hand tied behind your back?''

''I could. If I wanted to. As it happens, I have other duties. I am in the upper management of St. John Electronics!'' She paused. ''Or I was,'' she reflected.

''Don't quit on our account!''

''I'm not. I'm quitting for me.''

Hugh shook his head. ''This is insane. You can't just quit your job and move to an island you've never seen.''

''Of course I can. And I've seen quite a lot of the island. You drove me all the way across it.''

''In the dark. You don't know anything about it.''

''I don't need to know anything about it. Not yet. It isn't the island I need to learn about—it's me!''

Hugh put his head in his hands.

''Don't be melodramatic,'' Sydney said. ''It isn't going to hurt you. It might even be good for you,'' she added thoughtfully.

Hugh's head jerked up. ''What the hell does that mean?''

She shrugged, unconcerned. ''Nothing. Much.''

He narrowed his gaze. ''If you—''

''Oh, get over it. I just need to prove myself. And getting a job here will do that. I'm perfectly capable of running a business, for goodness' sake. I ran St. John's while Daddy was recovering from his heart attack.''

"Yeah, right."

Fire flashed in her eyes. "It didn't run itself for eight months, no matter what my father thinks!"

"You ran it and he never noticed?" Hugh said sarcastically.

"The doctors told me not to bring it up. Every time I mentioned St. John's, my father would get agitated. 'Who was taking care of business?' he'd ask. And if I tried to assure him I was, he got even more upset." She gripped her coffee mug so tightly her knuckles grew white. "Who was taking care of *me,* he'd ask. My father thinks women need to be taken care of. Always. So I stopped talking about it. I just did what needed to be done. I thought he'd understand when he got back to work that things hadn't just run themselves." She shook her head. "The more fool I."

She picked up another chicken wing and ran her tongue over her lips. Inwardly Hugh groaned.

"All right, don't believe me," Syd said, misunderstanding the reason for his moan. "But I've done all I'm going to do for St. John Electronics. I've got talents. I've got capabilities. I can manage someone else's company! I just need someone to hire me."

Hugh shook his head. "Just like that," he said dryly.

"What do you mean, just like that?"

"There aren't a lot of jobs for managing directors on Pelican Cay. We've got a population of somewhere around fifteen hundred, give or take a parakeet or two."

"Well, I'm sure someone will hire me."

"I'm not." Hugh was adamant about that. "You might be the greatest thing since sliced bread, but we don't need you on Pelican Cay." *I particularly don't need you.* "We don't do managing directors. We don't do hotshot female executives. So you'll just have to go somewhere else to find yourself."

She stared at him, opened her mouth, then she did it

again and looked at him pityingly. "As if you would know a hotshot executive of any sort even if it came up and bit you."

"I—"

"Just because *you* have nothing better to do than fish all day doesn't mean the rest of the world is the same."

"You ought to be glad I was."

"I said thank you."

"Did you? I don't remember."

They glared at each other. Then Hugh leaned forward suddenly so that all four chair legs landed on the floor with a thump. Abruptly he stood up, carried his dishes to the sink, and dumped them in.

"Since you're so determined to work," he said to her over his shoulder, "feel free." He jerked his head toward the overflowing sink. There were enough dirty dishes there to keep her busy awhile. "I'm sure you can *manage* that."

She sputtered indignantly. Served her right for being so snotty about his fishing trip. Deliberately Hugh yawned and headed toward the bedroom.

Behind him he heard her scramble to her feet. "Where am I going to sleep?"

"Not with me."

"I didn't imply—"

"There's a hammock on the porch." He cut her off, not wanting to discuss her sleeping arrangements any more than necessary. "Take that. Or you could try the sofa." He glanced at it. There was a sea kayak on it, balanced on several loads of laundry. "Maybe not the sofa."

"You don't have a guest room?"

"If you have a guest room, you get guests." Like his well-meaning parents or his interfering aunt Esme. He let them stay with Lachlan at the B&B. Far less meddlesome that way.

But Syd turned to look in the direction of his spare room. "What's that?"

"A mess."

It was his extra room. His "office" he called it. But it was more a closet than anything else. Lachlan had bunked there before he'd bought the Moonstone and the Mirabelle. Before that Great-Aunt Esme had commandeered it for her spring getaway one year and had expected him to clear it out for her. No one said no to Aunt Esme.

"We could clean it out," Sydney St. John said.

"No way."

"You don't have to. I will." Captain Ahab was back.

"No, you won't. It's almost midnight." He sighed when he could see she wasn't going to take no for an answer. "Look, okay. You take the bedroom tonight. I'll take the hammock. One night only." Then he turned and snapped his fingers for his dog. "C'mon, Belle. Time to hit the rack."

"By all means," Sydney St. John said. "Get your rest for another hard day fishing tomorrow."

Hugh's lips twitched. "I wish," he said. "Unfortunately, I'm flying to Jamaica in the morning."

Syd stared as if she hadn't heard him right. "You're—" long pause "—flying?"

Hugh dug into the back pocket of his shorts and pulled a business card out of his wallet. He flipped the card at her as he headed for the door.

"Maybe we're not all hotshot executives, but you're not the only one who can manage a business, Ms. St. John. Have fun cleaning up the dishes."

CHAPTER THREE

SHE had never done so many dishes in her life—and not just the ones in the sink.

Sydney did those as soon as Mr. "Fly Guy" McGillivray had banged out the door. Then, because she was still trying to work out the implications of that business card he'd flipped at her, she kept right on going. Heaven knew there were plenty of dirty dishes.

"Fly Guy" must do them once a week.

But the notion that he *flew*—that he actually had a business and supported himself by *flying* and apparently by doing other transportation-oriented things, as well—boggled her mind.

But that was what it said in big swooping letters on the business card: Fly Guy Island Charter. And below that in smaller type, the card proclaimed: "Whenever and wherever you want to go, call…Hugh McGillivray, Owner and Pilot."

Which meant, she supposed, that there was more to the man than dark good looks, hard muscles, kindness to dogs, a don't-bother-me-while-I'm-breathing attitude and a smart mouth?

She considered the possibility that he could just have the cards made to toss at people who crossed his path and commented on his lifestyle. But she doubted it. It would take too much effort. McGillivray didn't seem given to over-exertion.

He hadn't even bothered, in the end, to take a shower.

Instead he'd headed for the beach saying, "I'll take a swim instead."

He hadn't come back by the time she'd finished washing the dishes and had stripped the sheets off his bed and replaced them with clean ones. At least, she assumed they were clean ones as she'd found them in the same pile in the closet from which he'd taken the towel he'd given her.

There was a certain method to McGillivray's housekeeping. Dirty dishes were in the sink and on the countertop. Clean dishes were everywhere else. Dirty clothes were in a heap by the back door. Clean clothes and linens were in the closet in the bathroom and in heaps on the chairs. There were other piles, too, which she hadn't identified yet. She folded the clean clothes and took them into the bedroom. She left the dirty ones in a heap, but kicked them into the corner.

Now she padded out onto the front porch. She picked her way over the snorkles and swim fins and skirted the dog blanket and the portable cooler. Then she stood on the steps and let her eyes become accustomed to the darkness. There was a bit of moonlight spilling on the sea beyond some low bushes and across a narrow expanse of beach.

The sea where, presumably, McGillivray had gone swimming.

She didn't see him.

Just as well. She didn't want to think about him now. Didn't want to analyze the quickening sensation she felt every time she looked at Mr. Fly Guy McGillivray—or every time he looked at her.

It would be a distraction.

Syd didn't do distractions. She liked to focus. Zeroing in on a problem and assessing ways of overcoming it was her strength. Her father said that. Even Roland said it.

And now dear Roland had some firsthand experience with it, she thought grimly as she tipped her head back and let the night's soft breeze blow through her nearly dry hair.

The breeze soothed her, calmed her, made Roland and St. John Electronics seem as far away as another galaxy.

It really was gorgeous here—what she had seen of it. And quiet. Very different from Paradise Island. That had been glitz and glamour, casinos and jet-skiing and parasailing and lots of fast-paced to-ing and fro-ing. The only sound she could hear now was the soft rush of waves breaking on the shore.

She was tempted to walk down to the water, but she didn't see a path, and McGillivray's warning about the snakes was still fresh in her mind.

Were there really snakes?

She had no idea. With McGillivray, who could tell? His "gotcha" still rankled. Men ordinarily did not try to annoy Sydney St. John. On the contrary, usually they fell all over themselves trying to figure out what she wanted so they could do it.

Obviously not Fly Guy McGillivray. She studied the underbrush and thought she heard vague rustlings. She stayed where she was, studying his house instead.

It was a low-slung wood frame place of indeterminate age, whose color from what she could see on the porch seemed to be a sunny yellow. It sat on a rise overlooking the bushes and beach. In the distance through the trees she could see the lights of several more houses along a broad and gently curving cove. But they were scattered. There were a couple of larger places, probably inns, but even these were nothing like the string of high-rise hotels on Paradise Island.

Was Roland back there now? Or was he looking for her? Wherever he was, she hoped he was well on his way to panic. Serve him right.

If she hadn't jumped overboard, she realized, she would be in bed with Roland right now. The very thought made her shiver.

Or perhaps he wouldn't have expected theirs to be a *real* marriage.

No, that was the stuff of novels. Roland wouldn't have had the imagination to even think they might marry and not have sex. He would have married her for the business, but he would have expected his "conjugal rights" just as he had expected her to go along with his planned nuptials because it made good sense.

It would have been just another merger—only this time one of a physical sort. There would have been no passion. No love. No electricity. No spark.

An image of Hugh McGillivray flickered unbidden in her brain.

The sizzle between herself and McGillivray was exactly the opposite of the bloodless intellectual—and economic—merger that would have resulted from marrying Roland Carruthers.

Not that she was considering marrying McGillivray. Perish the thought!

Despite what Mr. Full-of-Himself Fly Guy implied, she had absolutely no interest in a relationship with him. Arrogant so-and-so! Syd wrapped her arms against her breasts and gave herself a little shake.

But the image didn't vanish. And she had to admit she was curious about that sizzle, those sparks. That wasn't something she'd ever felt before. Stirrings of interest, yes, now and then, when she'd encountered an attractive man.

But crackle, snap, pop? No. Never.

There had been times when Syd wondered if she had it in her to feel those things. Now she knew.

And her curiosity was piqued.

Would it happen again? She wanted to know.

Another reason to stay on Parakeet—no, Pelican—Cay. She would find a job and prove herself as she should have done years ago instead of trying to be the son her father had never had. And she would learn more about this intriguing sizzle between herself and McGillivray.

"You might be playing with fire," she warned herself aloud.

Well, yes. There was a danger of that. There was a danger to McGillivray. Even a novice to sizzle could see that.

But Syd believed in learning from experience. The more she could learn about "sizzle" now that it had finally happened to her, the better prepared she would be to appreciate it when it finally happened with the right man.

The breeze from the ocean touched her face and she smiled into it, looking forward, not back, relishing the challenge.

Then in the moonlight Syd caught sight of a man coming out of the water.

A lean hard man.

A graceful glistening man.

A naked man.

And she stared, mesmerized, as McGillivray stood for a moment silhouetted in the streaming silver light. Her mouth grew dry, her palms damp. Her heart kicked over in her chest, and an urgent sizzling heat curled downward from the middle of her belly. Flames of desire licked at her.

If the thought of going to bed with Roland had left her somewhere between indifferent and nonplused, the thought of sharing a bed with McGillivray was a whole different story.

She held herself absolutely still, drinking in the sight of him and at the same time trying to get a grip on her buzzing brain and rampaging hormones. There was sizzle, all right. And sparks and fireworks and, if she weren't careful, a whole conflagration.

That was why she needed to stay. To learn to control the fire.

Tomorrow. And in days to come. Right now she was going to bed. Alone.

She'd made enough life-changing decisions for one day.

HUGH loved his hammock. As long as he didn't have to spend the night in it. It was great for lazy afternoon naps.

It was fine for wiling away a summer evening drinking a beer and reading a book.

But nights—whole nights—got long. Very long. Especially if a guy couldn't sleep.

Hugh couldn't sleep.

Ordinarily he slept like the proverbial baby. "It's all that innocence and virtue," he always claimed.

"All that beer more like," his sister, Molly, always countered.

But neither beer nor virtue nor a good long swim had taken him to dreamland tonight.

Maybe, Hugh reasoned as he tried for the hundredth time to find a comfortable spot, it was just too damn hot. Or maybe there wasn't enough support for his back. Or maybe it was not being in his own bed that was keeping him awake.

More likely, he decided grimly, it was who was in his bed instead of him that was making him turn over and over like a chicken revolving on a spit. It was well past three in the morning and he'd barely shut his eyes.

Every time he did, visions of Sydney St. John lying between his sheets popped into his brain. He ground his teeth and shifted again. And again. And again. The swim should have tired him out. It certainly should have taken the edge off his desire.

He wasn't a teenager anymore, for heaven's sake! He was an adult—a man in control of his urges.

Finally, in a fit of irritation, he flipped over with enormous force—and flung himself right out onto the porch floor.

"Damn it!"

Belle, who had leaped off her blanket by his feet, whined and looked at him warily. Then she took hold of the corner of her blanket and pulled it away from the hammock. He'd get away from him, too, if he could.

"Hell," he muttered, rubbing the shoulder on which he'd landed, then hauling himself to his feet. He eyed the still-

swaying hammock with distaste. No point trying it again.
It wouldn't work.

He might as well head over to the shop. There was a
couch there. But even more likely to put him to sleep was
the pile of paperwork he had been avoiding for the past
couple of weeks. If anything could knock him out, he knew
from boring experience, it would be that.

Hugh bent down to scratch Belle's ears. "Go back to
sleep. I won't bother you anymore." Then, yawning, he
padded across the porch and opened the screen door to the
kitchen.

He flipped on the light—and stared in amazement. The
place was spotless. There wasn't a dirty dish in sight.

He grinned. So snooty Miss Sydney could turn to, when
she was challenged. Somehow he wasn't surprised. Any
woman who had the guts to jump overboard in the middle
of the damn ocean—

Hugh shook his head, reminding himself that she was
seriously wacko. She had to be to have done that. And she
was even crazier to think that she was going to get a managing director's job on Pelican Cay.

She'd just been babbling over dinner, annoyed—and
rightly so, he admitted—that she'd been wasting her time
in a job where she was obviously capable but not appre-
ciated. He didn't blame her for wanting to prove herself.

He just didn't want her proving herself here.

Well, he didn't have to worry about that. Only his
brother Lachlan's inn-and-resort business was extensive
and complex enough to require a managing director. And
Lachlan did that himself. All the rest of the islanders ran
their own smaller operations by themselves, too. Multina-
tional corporations were not thick on Pelican Cay's sandy
beaches as Sydney St. John would discover damn quick.

And then she'd be on her way.

The thought cheered him enough that he took down the
sugar bowl where he kept a stash of dollars and coins,
dumped it all on the table and scrawled a quick note: "Use

this to get yourself some clothes. If you need more money, give them this note. I'll cover for you. H.''

Neither place would be what she was used to—not if the beaded dress was anything to go by. But that would just encourage her to leave even sooner. In the meantime she could wear something of his.

He glanced around and realized that all his clean clothes were gone. The dirty ones were still there—in a pile in the corner—but the ones he'd washed last weekend were no longer in the chair.

''Hell's bells.'' She'd obviously taken it upon herself to clean them up, too. Probably took them in the bedroom and put them in the dresser drawers like some obsessive neat freak. Which meant he was going to have to go into the bedroom to get something to wear.

She was asleep on his bed.

Long, bare limbs silvery in the moonlight slanting through the blinds, Sydney St. John lay on her back, one arm flung out, the other across her middle. A cloud of dark hair framed her face.

What a face, Hugh thought. The hell with managing director jobs, the woman should be a cover model.

He ought to know. He had flown enough of them to and from photo shoots all over the islands. He knew cover-model-quality cheekbones when he saw them. He had seen—and kissed—his share of cover-model-quality lips, too.

Sydney St. John had them both. And even that scattering of freckles he'd seen earlier wouldn't have deterred photographers. On the contrary, it would have enchanted them, made her look ''approachable,'' ''wholesome,'' ''all-American.'' Hugh knew all the adjectives. He knew they were all true.

In sleep, he admitted, even her stubborn chin had something to recommend it.

Then, as he stood watching her, her lips twitched and twisted. She frowned and muttered. Her long legs scissored and she rolled onto her side, clutching the pillow against her breasts like a shield.

"No!" she said fiercely. "I won't!"

Hugh backed away. No point in eavesdropping. Especially when he didn't want to hear her distress. He jerked open a drawer. His clothes were all there, folded neatly. Now it was his turn to mutter under his breath.

"No! I said, no!" Her voice was agitated.

Hurriedly Hugh pawed through the stack of shirts, grabbed one, got a pair of shorts and boxers out of the drawer below, started to shut them, then pulled out clothes for her, as well. Then, without looking back, he left the room.

"No!" Her voice followed him. He yanked on his clothes, trying to ignore her. But Hugh had always been a sucker for damsels in distress. He raked a hand through his hair, cracked his knuckles and headed for the door. Belle met him there, cocking her head to look at him worriedly.

"Not our business," Hugh told her firmly. It wasn't. And not their problem, either. "C'mon, Belle."

From the bedroom he heard, "Stop it! No, I won't! I won't!"

And there was a loud bang.

"Oh, God! Now what?" He hurried back to the bedroom expecting to find her on the floor.

She wasn't. Instead she'd twisted around and punched the wall so hard there was a crumbling hole in the plaster.

"For crying out loud." Hugh crossed the room as she rolled back over. Her eyes opened and she saw him looming next to the bed.

"Get away!" she shouted and took a roundhouse swing that caught him in the eye.

"Ow! Bloody hell!"

"Ohmigod!" She stared at him, dazed and astonished. Her breaths came in quick gasps as she rubbed her hand vaguely and finally seemed to realize where she was. Then her shoulders slumped, her eyelids shuttered.

"Oh," she said, "it's you."

"Yeah," he said dryly. "It's me." Carefully, tentatively, he touched his eye. And winced.

"Sorry," she muttered, wincing, too. "I didn't mean... I was...dreaming."

"Nothing personal, then?" Hugh said lightly, steeling himself against feeling sorry for her, against reaching out and hauling her into his arms as his instincts wanted to. Fortunately his sense of self-preservation was stronger.

Damn but she packed a wallop.

"Sorry," she muttered again. "I thought you were..."

"Roland?"

She nodded, shaking, wrapping her arms across her chest, then rubbed her bruised knuckles against her lips and grimaced.

"You all right? Maybe you need a doctor."

"I don't need a doctor." Her eyes flashed. Her chin lifted. "I'm fine."

"Right. Sure you are. You're probably having a delayed reaction. Shock."

She started to deny it, then shrugged. She turned to look at the hole she'd put in the wall. "Did I do that?"

"Unless it was a snake," Hugh said.

Her eyes snapped back to meet his, wide as dinner plates, then they looked wildly around the room.

"Kidding," Hugh said.

Sydney shuddered. "Not funny."

"Probably not." But a whole lot safer than reaching for her and comforting her. He jammed his hands into the pockets of his shorts. "You're tense. How about a little something to make you relax?"

"What?" She raised a brow. "You mean like a beer?"

"If you want," he said offhandedly. "But I was thinking of something else. My aunt Esme swore by it. Used to give it to us all the time. Whenever we were twitchy."

"Twitchy?"

"Upset. Couldn't sleep."

"Oh. Your aunt Esme did that?" She looked at him suspiciously as if he were making her up.

He nodded. "My father's aunt, really. Esme had a cure for everything. She always knew best." He shook his head ruefully at all his memories of bossy, domineering Aunt Esme. "I'll fix you some." Anything to get out of standing there watching her breasts move beneath the cotton of her borrowed T-shirt. Hastily he headed for the kitchen.

Bare feet slapped on the floor following him. "What is it? What are you making?"

"Never mind. You can't watch. If you do, it won't work. Go back to bed. I'll bring it in."

For a minute he thought she would refuse. She eyed him warily. "Why won't it work?"

"I don't know. That's what she always said. My dad said it was because she put eye of newt in it."

"Eye of newt?" Syd looked appalled.

Hugh grinned. "My dad's a doctor. He thinks Esme's a quack."

"And that's why you're fixing me her cure-all?"

"I'm fixing it so you can sleep. Go back to bed. No eye of newt," he promised.

The corners of her mouth tipped up. Then she sighed and shrugged. "All right." She gave another shudder. "I just hope it works."

Hugh hoped she'd be asleep by the time he heated it and brought it in to her.

Of course she wasn't. When he returned she was back in bed with the small bedside lamp on. He handed her a mug. She sniffed it suspiciously.

"Smells like eye of newt."

"Nope. It's lizard. Drink up."

Sydney choked. She looked at him, aghast, then heaved a sigh. "You are so juvenile." Gripping the mug, she brought it to her lips and took a cautious sip. "It's hot." She touched her tongue to her lips. "It's just milk," she decided, then tasted again. "And something else."

"Lizard," Hugh repeated. "And a few spiders."

"Right. And snakes, I'm sure."

"Nope." He shook his head. "Aunt Esme was afraid of snakes."

"I don't believe you even have an aunt Esme. You put rum in this," she said accusingly.

He shrugged. "Figured you were old enough to drink."

Sydney nodded and took another, deeper swallow, then settled back against the pillows. "It's good." She smiled up at him. "Thank you."

The smile had him stepping back away from the bed. He nodded quickly. "Glad you like it. Drink it all up, then shut out the light and go back to sleep. I'll see you tomorrow—well, today, really—afternoon."

"Afternoon?"

"I'm gonna head over to the shop."

"Now?" She stared at him.

He shrugged and swallowed a yawn. "Why not? Not getting any sleep here." He arched his aching back. "Hammock's not all it's cracked up to be."

She winced. "I'm sorry. When I angled to sleep in your bed, I didn't realize you were a working man who really needed your sleep." She actually sounded slightly abashed. "I'll take the hammock."

"Don't worry about it. I can catch a few winks on the couch in the office." He turned to go.

"What about your eye?" she demanded. "You should have ice for your eye."

"I don't need ice."

"You'll have a black eye in the morning if you don't. I'll get you some." And damned if she didn't start to get out of bed.

"The hell you will," Hugh said, blocking her way. "I'll get my own ice, *if* I decide I need any."

Their gazes locked, dueled. When he and Lachlan were little they'd had these pretend swords that lit up with sparks whenever they hit each other. Hugh felt like he was seeing those same sparks now. He gave his head a fierce shake. And grimaced because his eye did hurt.

"I'll put some ice on it," he muttered, "if you just shut up and go to bed."

Once more she looked as if she might refuse, but then she tucked her feet back under the sheet and nodded. "All right." She paused. "Thank you."

"You're welcome," he said with equal politeness. Their gazes met once more—and lingered. Finally Hugh dragged his away, turned and started out of the room.

"McGillivray?"

He stopped. "What?"

"I...I really am grateful. I'll fix the hole in the wall."

He'd forgotten about the damn hole. "Don't worry about it."

"I will. I—"

"Go to sleep, St. John," he said firmly, and walked out, shutting the door behind him.

But when he got to the porch, he didn't feel as if he should leave. What if she had another nightmare? She'd hit the wall last time. What if Esme's potion didn't calm her down? What if she panicked? Got disoriented?

Hugh sat down on the porch swing. It was even less comfortable than the hammock. He went back into the house and sat on one of the kitchen chairs. No good, either. He made himself a bed on the pile of laundry in the corner on the floor. Not too bad. He rolled onto his side so he could see the bedroom light beneath the door.

Belle padded over and stuck her face down next to his and looked at him quizzically.

"Don't ask," Hugh muttered.

Belle wandered back outside and settled onto her bed. From the bedroom he heard the bed creak. The light went off.

Hugh glanced at his watch—4:00. Swell. He shifted. He stretched. He sighed. He squirmed.

Sydney slept.

At least he assumed she did. He didn't. He was getting too damn old for floors. And his eye throbbed. He got some ice, put it in a plastic bag and held it against his face. That was what he was doing when the shouting started again.

"Damn it to hell!" Hugh tossed the ice bag into the sink and stalked into the bedroom.

Syd was thrashing on the bed, arms and legs churning.

"Wake up!" he shouted from across the room.

She sat up abruptly and stared at him, dazed. "What? Why are you yelling at me?"

"I'm not the one yelling, sweetheart. That was you."

"Oh." Her head sagged forward and she thrust her hands through her hair. "Oh, I'm sorry. I—"

"Move over."

Her hands dropped. Her body straightened abruptly and she looked up at him. "What did you say?"

"You heard me." He stalked across the room and flung himself onto the bed beside her.

"What are you doing?" Her voice was high-pitched.

"What do you think?"

Now she really did look stricken.

"Relax." Hugh sighed, pushing her back onto the bed and flinging an arm across her to pin her there. "I'm not going to have my wicked way with you. I'm just going to try to convince your brain that Roland isn't here, so you can get some sleep."

"But...you'll be here," she pointed out.

"So what?"

"So maybe I won't be able to sleep then, either."

"Maybe not," Hugh said grimly. "But I hope to God I will."

CHAPTER FOUR

SHE didn't know if Hugh slept or not.

But despite her protestations to the contrary, Sydney fell asleep almost at once. For reasons she hesitated to examine too closely, the solid warmth of McGillivray's hard body next to hers, the possessive feel of his arm around her and the steady sound of his breathing so close that it might have been her own worked a magic she wouldn't have believed possible.

One minute she was astonished at his presumption—and the next she was sound asleep.

Best of all, it had been a dreamless sleep.

For the first time that night when she'd closed her eyes, Roland hadn't come back to haunt her. In fact, all the stresses of life at St. John Electronics had been blessedly absent. Even her father had stayed away.

When she finally opened her eyes, it was to find the sun already high in the sky. And even then it was the sound of youthful voices, laughing and talking as they passed the open window, that finally awakened her.

She heard them and the sound of the surf, she felt the lazy breeze of an overhead fan and not the hum of air conditioning and for a few seconds she couldn't imagine where she was.

And then it all came back. Paradise Island, the Butler buyout, the "bonding" yacht trip, Roland's wedding announcement, her surreptitious plunge overboard and desperate swim to reach the boat she'd spied in the distance.

McGillivray.

Her eyes flew open. She sat up to look around wildly.
She was alone in the room. Alone in the bed.
Now.
But she hadn't spent the night alone. She remembered
that, too. McGillivray had been there. McGillivray had slept
with her.
Syd had never *slept* with a man before. Gone to bed with,
yes. Twice. The more fool she. Neither had been exactly
memorable.
No. Not true. She remembered them well enough. She
just didn't want to.
They had both been unpleasant experiences, albeit for
different reasons. The first time—an eager youthful fum-
bling that had seemed more awkward and painful than ful-
filling—had made her determined to try again "with the
right man." But her second experience four years ago,
when she'd actually thought she was in love with Nicholas
and he'd been in love with her being the heir to St. John
Electronics, had left her with no desire to try a third.
At least Roland had got into St. John's on his own merits,
even if he did think subsequently that marrying her would
be a good business decision for both of them.
Syd supposed she ought to be grateful for that.
Certainly there had been no zing or sizzle between them.
She had never once envisioned—or desired—to experience
lovemaking with Roland. And that had been fine with her.
There would be time enough for that sort of thing when
she had found the right man, married him and wanted to
have children. Sex for its own sake seemed highly over-
rated.
Then.
Somehow McGillivray didn't inspire the same sublime
disinterest.
And yet she had actually *slept* with him there.
Weird.
Sydney couldn't quite bend her mind around that. It
probably had something to do with the rum and whatever

else he put in that concoction he'd made for her. But it wasn't the concoction that had made her sleep.

She swallowed, feeling a tingle of lingering awareness even now. It energized her, gave her purpose. It was the first day of the rest of her life—her *new* life.

She bounced out of bed and got to work.

McGillivray's house was actually quite wonderful once you got past the mess and the clutter. It wasn't palatial like the Long Island home she'd grown up in or the sumptuous penthouse her father kept in New York. Both of those were elegant and opulent and a tribute to her mother's decorating taste.

McGillivray's place was a tribute to the thrift shops and the hand-me-down school of interior decoration. But it was bright and breezy and the view of the nearly deserted beach and turquoise sea could not be surpassed.

Besides that, it felt homey, warm and welcoming. Syd had never lived in a place that felt homey and welcoming.

Sun streamed in as soon as she opened the wooden blinds. But even beyond the sunlight, there were colors everywhere—in the mismatched furniture—the lumpy futon with its bright-blue cover, the wicker rocker with its palm-tree-print cushion and the pillows scattered about. It was a room clearly designed for comfort and function with no thought at all given to style.

And that gave it a style all its own.

Syd liked the style. It was fresh and open and as brash as McGillivray himself. It would be even better if someone dealt with all the clutter.

So she did.

Straightening and sorting, making piles and making decisions about what stayed and what went energized her, focused her. He obviously hated doing it himself. So she would do it for him. She started in his spare room, making it hers, then moved quickly from one room to another, sorting and shelving and straightening. And while she did so, she did the same to her life, articulating her talents aloud

while she shelved his books, reminding herself of her ac-
complishments while she lined up all his various engine
parts, enumerating her goals while she swept and scrubbed
the floors, shook the rugs and dusted everything in sight.

And once she had blitzed her way through his house,
making it tidy and presentable and remarkably *un*cluttered—if you ignored the pile of stuff she had no idea what
to do with and had stacked neatly in the spare room and
shut the door—she was ready to do the same for herself.

She took a quick shower, found the clean T-shirt and
pair of shorts McGillivray had left her and, fortunately, a
belt to hold them up with. Since McGillivray's amenities
didn't run to hair dryers, she simply pulled her long dark
hair back into a ponytail and wrapped a rubber band around
it. She hadn't worn her hair in a ponytail since she was ten
years old.

When she was eleven, her father had sent her to the
Swiss convent school her mother had attended, to learn to
be a lady.

"Ladies," Sister Ermintrude, who was in charge of de-
portment, informed her, "do not look like horses."

The ponytail had gone.

Now a woman she barely recognized stared back at Syd
from the mirror.

The always professional, always perfect Margaret St.
John—with her sophisticated demeanor, her skillfully applied makeup, neatly groomed hair and quietly elegant
clothes—was gone.

The woman in the mirror looked like a different person
altogether. Younger. Earthier. More elemental.

Sunburned, in fact, Syd thought, wrinkling her already-
beginning-to-peel nose. And still freckled. For years she
had treated them as blemishes. Now they defied her to try.

She cocked her head and considered herself. The woman
in the mirror cocked her head right back. Syd smiled tentatively. So did the woman. It began as a cool professional

smile, but it didn't remain one. It widened, grew quirkier, turned into a grin.

The woman grinning back wasn't wholly unknown. In fact, Syd felt rather as if she had unexpectedly met an old friend. A girl she used to know—and like. A self she had buried under layers of polish and civility. The girl who had been Syd, not the woman who had become Margaret.

It seemed fitting somehow.

"Ready or not," she told the mirror and the world at large, "here I come."

There were a few people on the beach—sunbathing and swimming and a few batting a volleyball around—but it was nearly empty compared to the beach by the hotel where she and Roland had stayed. It was prettier, though. The sand was almost pink and very powdery between her toes as she walked out onto the beach to get a look around.

Last night's perception of the lay of the land turned out to be reasonably accurate. McGillivray's low-slung, yellow, wood frame cottage sat on the crest of a low dune overlooking the beach. There were other houses dotted along the same ridge, masked by the same line of palms and other foliage that shaded McGillivray's. And quite a way down the beach there seemed to be a larger building, an inn, she guessed, because outside it a game of volleyball was going on, and several people sat beneath beach umbrellas, and a few more were paddling about in the water. But between where she stood and the inn, she could count no more than a dozen other sunbathers and swimmers.

Paradise, she thought. Unspoiled. Gorgeous. It invited her to bask in its unhurried charm.

But she couldn't. Not yet. She had work to do. Clothes to buy. A job to find. A future to discover.

McGillivray had left money and a note on the table. She tucked it into the pocket of her shorts and, wearing a pair of his too-large-for-her flip-flops, set off down the potholed road toward where she hoped to find the town.

The further she got from the ocean, the less breeze there

was and the hotter Syd became. McGillivray's T-shirt stuck to her back. She could feel a line of perspiration trickling down between her breasts. It was a relief when the narrow road through the foliage opened out onto a large well-groomed field with soccer goals at either end. Beside it was a large Quonset hut and a new frame building, and right next to the road, overlooking both, loomed a sculpture of the most amazing collection of junk Syd had ever seen.

It rose at least twelve feet in the air, and it was made of everything from railroad ties and driftwood spars to plastic sunscreen bottles and beer kegs. Sea glass and aluminum foil alike hung from fishing line and glittered and swayed. In its outstretched arm, it held a Junkanoo T-shirt. A pair of gigantic sunglasses were settled on a soda bottle nose, and a battered visor that looked more like a crown with its woven straw points, shielded the sculpture's "face" from the sun.

Syd stared up at it, astonished and laughing at the same time. It looked like where all McGillivray's clutter went to die.

"First time you've met him?" an amused voice asked.

Syd turned. A woman about her own age was wiping her face on a bandanna as she came toward Syd from the Quonset hut.

"Yes. He's amazing."

"He is. We call him the *King of the Beach*. My sister-in-law made him. *Makes* him," the woman corrected herself. "He's a work in progress. Like all men." She grinned.

Syd grinned back. "He's better than most."

"Oh, yeah." The woman stuffed the bandanna in the pocket of her shorts. They were men's like the ones Syd was wearing, and peeked out below an oversize orange T-shirt that, had it not been faded almost to gold, would have clashed furiously with a riot of carroty curls. The curls, Syd suspected, were natural, and exactly the sort that hundreds of women would have spent hours in a salon to accomplish. This woman had them tucked beneath a grease-streaked purple sweatband, which was entirely functional.

"You must be Hugh's friend," the woman said.

Syd blinked. "Um, well, yes. But how did you—"

A grin flashed. The woman wiped a slightly greasy hand on the side of her shorts, then stuck it out. "He told me. I'm Molly."

"Molly?"

"McGillivray. His sister," Molly clarified cheerfully. "For my sins. When he left this morning, he said he had a friend staying with him. He said I was supposed to 'stay away from his place so his friend could have peace and quiet.'" Molly's tongue traced a circle inside her cheek, and Syd could see her lips twitch as she tried not to grin. "I wonder why."

Syd wasn't sure what to reply to that. "I had a hard day yesterday," she said finally.

Molly laughed and raised her brows. "Thanks to Hugh?"

"Not exactly." But she could hardly explain what had happened.

Molly didn't seem to care, anyway. "What a dark horse!" she said cheerfully. "He never said a word. But I'm so glad!"

"Glad?"

"That he's moved on."

Syd didn't have a clue what Hugh's sister was talking about. She was also fairly sure she couldn't say that. So she settled for saying, "I don't think he mentioned you, either, I'm afraid."

Molly shrugged. "Most guys don't talk a lot about their sisters. Did you give him the black eye?"

Syd felt color rise in her cheeks. "Accidentally," she admitted. "I bumped into him."

Molly nodded knowingly. "Right. I won't ask. You don't have to tell. So, are you going to marry him?"

"*What?*"

Molly laughed. "There are some things I do ask. I'm blunt. Everybody says so. That McGillivray girl has no tact, they say." She shrugged, her eyes twinkling. "And it's true. But who cares? He's my brother. I love him, and I want the best for him. You seem to know how to deal with him."

Syd shook her head, still reeling. "I don't think I know anything of the sort."

Molly shrugged. "Well, you made a good start. He's very careful of you. Protects you and all that. So what about it? Are you?"

Clearly Hugh's sister wasn't going to be put off.

"We're discussing it," Syd said enigmatically. Well, they had discussed marriage, though not exactly with the results that Molly clearly hoped for!

But apparently her words satisfied. "Good enough for me," Molly said. "At least you didn't say you were 'just friends.' That's lame."

Having been tempted to do just that, Syd was glad she'd restrained herself. "But sometimes people are just friends," she pointed out.

"Of course. But you're not. You've got to be pretty special or Hugh wouldn't have invited you to live with him."

"I'm not exactly *living* with him. I'm staying with him for a while."

"It's a start. Hugh's never asked a woman to live with him before. It means he's getting past Carin."

Carin? "Who's Carin?"

Molly clapped her hand over her mouth. "See? No tact at all. I shouldn't have said anything." She hesitated. "Oh, hell. You should know…" Molly sucked in a breath and then blurted, "Carin Campbell. She's an artist. A really good artist. Heaps of talent. She has shows in Miami and New York and Santa Fe. But she lives here on Pelican Cay. She owns Carin's Cottage, a gallery and gift shop just down the road." She jerked her head in the direction of the town.

"I see," Syd said, but she didn't.

She still didn't know what Carin had to do with Hugh McGillivray. Obviously there were issues, but were they bigger issues than between him and Lisa?

"So what happened?" she asked finally when Molly didn't say anything else.

"Nothing."

"Nothing? I don't understand."

Molly shrugged. "Carin got married a couple of years ago. She and Nathan Wolfe."

"The photographer Nathan Wolfe?"

"You know him?"

"Of him," Syd said. "I own some of his books. He's terrifically talented."

"He's also terrifically handsome. And in love with Carin. And the father of her daughter." Molly sighed. "Hugh never had a chance."

"Ah." Now Syd did see. "He loved her."

"He never said so," Molly replied her quickly. "He never would. Not Hugh. It was always no pressure with Hugh. He was 'just friends' with Carin for years. Always keeping it cool. Letting her set the pace. And she did. She walked right into Nathan's arms." Molly shook her head sadly. "I mean, she made Nathan sweat. But not because of Hugh. Poor sod."

"But if he never said, are you sure…?"

"He's my brother. Of course I'm sure." Molly was adamant. "It's just who he is. Hugh's always easy. It's always all fun and games with him. He's Mr. Devil-May-Care personified. At least, that's what he'd like you to think. But then, I'm sure you know that even better than I do," Molly said.

"Um…oh. Yes. Of course," Syd managed weakly.

"So yes, he cared about Carin. But not as much as he cares about you."

"What?" Syd's eyes widened. "What do you mean by that?"

"I told you. He warned me off. Told me to let you be."

Molly gave her a conspiratorial smile. "He protected you. That's the very first time he's *ever* done that. I mean *obviously* done it. So—" she beamed "—things are looking up. I'm really glad you're here."

Syd was beginning to wonder just how glad she was. Hugh McGillivray seemed to have far too many women in his life. She changed the subject before she said something she would regret.

"Hugh mentioned a place to get clothes here on the island?" she said. "Erica's?"

"Yeah. It's a boutique. Or as close to a boutique as we're likely to get. Lots of trendy stuff. Tourists love it. Some of the locals do, too. I don't have much use for that sort of stuff." She wrinkled her nose. "I did when I was teaching, though God knows why. I used to come home with lots worse things than grease and motor oil on me."

"You get a lot of grease and motor oil on you now?" Today's appearance wasn't a one-off, then?

"Every day, now that I work here," Molly said happily. She jerked her head back at the shop. "I'm Hugh's mechanic—and his copilot. That's the fun stuff. I also get all the lousy jobs, though, like answering the phone and dealing with the bookwork and the scheduling and the accounting and billing. Yuck stuff like that."

Syd raised her brows at the description. "Accounting's not yuck. I like it."

Molly looked horrified. "You *like* putting little numbers in little boxes?"

Syd grinned. "Love it. You put all those little numbers in all those little boxes and add them all up and they come out just right. It's beautiful."

Molly looked at her as if she'd lost her mind. "Dear God."

Syd hesitated, then thought, why not? "If you don't like it, maybe I could do it for you."

Molly seemed dumbstruck at the offer. She gave her head a little shake. "What did you say?"

"I said if you don't like—"

"No, I heard you. I just don't believe it. You are volunteering to do the accounting?"

"And the billing if you want."

"*If I want?* Oh, yes. Oh yes, oh yes, oh yes! I could kiss your feet!" Molly would have grabbed her, greasy hands and all, and swung her enthusiastically if Syd hadn't sidestepped fast.

"Not necessary," Syd said. "But I need to do a little shopping first. I have to get some clothes."

"Girly stuff?" Molly said doubtfully. She cast an approving glance at McGillivray's shorts and T-shirt that Syd was wearing.

"Tasteful stuff. That fits," Syd added with a grimace downward at the baggy shorts and shirt she wore.

Molly shrugged. "To each her own. Go to Erica's then. Or The Cotton Shoppe. Carin buys some stuff there. Just head downhill. You'll come to Erica's first. The Cotton Shoppe is beside the bakery. You'll be able to smell it."

"Sounds good." She started to head that way.

"And then you'll come back and do the billing?" Molly called after her urgently, as if to remind her.

"And then I'll come back and do the billing," Syd promised. "Maybe I can work it into a real job."

Molly looked interested. "You want a real job?"

"Yes. I do. I—"

"Then it *is* serious with you and Hugh. I thought so!"

Syd knew she should object and say that McGillivray had nothing to do with it, but she didn't think Molly would believe her. And maybe that was just as well.

After all, wasn't that what he wanted people to think? If Lisa was supposed to believe that Syd was his girlfriend, it would help if everyone else thought there was something there, too. She felt a little guilty misleading his sister, but McGillivray himself would probably be pleased.

"I'll be back in an hour or so," she promised Molly. "I

need to pick up some plaster, too. Hardware store in town?''

Molly nodded and gave directions for that, too. ''How about picking up some sandwiches at the bakery on your way back?'' Molly dug deep into one of her pockets and pulled out a wad of dollar bills and thrust them at Syd. ''My treat.''

As she had no money of her own, Syd was obliged to accept. She stuffed the bills in her pocket, determinedly ignoring the grease. After all, she consoled herself, they were McGillivray's shorts she was wearing.

WITH luck she was gone.

It was nearly dusk when Hugh set the seaplane down on the smooth water just beyond the island's small harbor and savored, as he always did, the sight of Pelican Town silhouetted in the coppery light. But there was a wariness in his gut tonight as he brought the plane into its mooring.

All day long he'd done his best to put Sydney St. John out of him mind—and she wouldn't go.

He'd even left Doc Rasmussen to get his own supplies while he went to the beach and then to one of the local hangouts where he knew there were plenty of lovely ladies, determined to think about all the women he had yet to meet.

And he still couldn't shake the memory of spending the night with Syd.

And when was the last time he'd spent the night with a woman and hadn't made love to her? He might have been seven and sleeping in a tent in his backyard with his brother and the kids next door, one of whom had been a girl.

But he'd slept with Sydney St. John last night and he hadn't touched her. Not like that. He'd only held her, doing his best to protect her from the demons plaguing her dreams.

And he thought he'd succeeded. At least she hadn't twisted and grimaced and moaned in his arms. Instead she'd closed her eyes almost at once. Then slowly he'd felt her body relax, the tautness in her muscles ease, her breathing slow. And then she'd sighed and snuggled up to him and smiled.

Snuggled!

And heaven help him, he'd snuggled back. Something else he couldn't ever remember doing before.

But that was then. She'd better be gone when he got home tonight.

Of course, in the first place he'd figured she'd stay two or three days—long enough to shake up Carruthers and long enough to make sure Lisa knew he wasn't interested in her. But after last night he'd changed his mind. He wanted her gone.

He'd picked up a couple of business weeklies while he was in Kingston today and they both had articles about the St. Johns and they both quoted the "savvy and sensible, supremely articulate Ms. St. John."

They'd called her Margaret St. John, but one of them had her picture. Hugh knew that face. He'd seen that body—the one beneath the slim professional power suit.

He didn't want to spend another night with it nearby tempting him, he thought as he and Doc Rasmussen unloaded all the medical supplies into the dinghy. There was just so much of that sort of thing a healthy red-blooded man could endure.

Maurice Sawyer was waiting to transport the supplies to the clinic, his taxi parked at the foot of the dock. He sauntered up the dock to meet them, glancing at his watch as he came.

"Sorry we're late," Hugh said.

"I just bet you is," Maurice said, a grin wreathing his face. "You go on," he said to Hugh cheerfully. "I reckon you be in a big hurry." He clapped Hugh on the shoulder, then gave him a broad wink and a grin.

Hugh felt a sense of foreboding. "Why am I in a hurry?"

The whites of Maurice's eyes shone in the darkness. "You forget your pretty lady then?"

Doc ambled up carrying a load of supplies. "Pretty lady? What pretty lady?" he asked.

"Hugh's lady. She's somethin'," he told Doc appreciatively. "Long long legs. An' curves. Real nice curves. Sweet as they come, too."

Obviously, they weren't talking about Syd, then. Hugh narrowed his gaze. "You talked to her?"

Maurice nodded. "Met her at the bakery."

"I thought you were distracted today," Doc reflected. "Hell, we didn't have to stay gone this long. Why didn't you say you had a lady waiting for you?"

Hugh shrugged. "You hired me. Your time is my time. It didn't matter. She knew I was going to be gone." The truth and nothing but.

"But you could have brought her along," Doc said earnestly. "We had room."

"I didn't want to bring her along!"

Both men blinked at his sharp tone.

Hugh raked a hand through his hair and ran his tongue over his lips. "It's just— She had a hard day yesterday. Didn't get a lot of sleep."

Both men nodded gravely and suppressed grins.

Hugh gritted his teeth. "And I thought she ought to get some," he said, ignoring the fact that his face was burning like some teenager's.

Damn it! He *never* got embarrassed talking about women. What was it about this one that was so completely complicating his life?

"It's not a big deal," he muttered.

Doc eyed him for a long moment doubtfully, then shrugged. "Whatever you say." He shifted the box in his arms, then carried it down to Maurice's taxi and put it in the back. "Go on now, though. You've done enough. You don't have to hang around now and help unload."

"It's my job."

"It's not," Doc said. "And your lady is waiting."

"Yeah. Reckon she be back by now," Maurice said.

"Back?" Hugh looked up. "She left?"

Maurice nodded. "Went with Amby. He took her in his boat this afternoon."

"Did he?" Hugh felt suddenly heartened.

Amby Higgs ran one of the water taxis that took tourists sightseeing and over to Spanish Wells and mostly to the main island to catch scheduled airlines to the States.

So she had come to her senses and gone back to Daddy after all.

Hugh shoved his hands into his pockets and took a deep breath. "Maybe I will mosey on along," he said. "Grab some takeout at The Grouper, then head home."

Doc grinned. "You do that." Both he and Maurice waved Hugh off encouragingly.

Feeling immeasurably lighter, Hugh set off down the quay, Belle at his heels.

"Don't do nothin' I wouldn't do!" Maurice called after him.

"No fear."

Belle jumped in the jeep. Hugh followed and flicked on the ignition. He looked around. Something was odd. Different.

It took him a moment to realize what it was.

No Lisa.

For the first time in weeks Lisa Milligan hadn't been waiting at the dock to smile and simper at him. She hadn't followed him up the quay hanging on his arm, telling him what she'd cooked and how much he'd enjoy it and how happy she was to have him back.

He was free.

The ruse had worked.

And while he might have hurt her feelings, he was sure he hadn't hurt them as badly as he would have if he'd had to brush her off another, blunter way.

And all he'd had to suffer for it was the sharp edge of Sydney St. John's tongue—and a night of sharing a bed with her.

"Not a bad deal," he told Belle as he stomped on the gas.
At least, that's what he thought.
Until he got home.

CHAPTER FIVE

SOMETHING else was different, too.

Hugh could sense it the minute he got out of the Jeep behind the house. But in the dusk everything looked the same.

And yet…

He shrugged and gave his head a quick shake. Sometimes he felt a brief disorientation on solid ground after a flight. Maybe that was it. That and having had less than three hours' sleep last night, thanks to Ms. Sydney St. John.

Well, tonight he'd make up for it. Tonight, thanks to Ms. St. John's cooperation, he would spend the evening eating his grouper and peas and rice in peace—with no Lisa hovering. And then he would watch a film or read a book, maybe go for a swim, take Belle for a long walk, then fall into bed—after he'd changed the sheets so no lingering scents distracted him—and have a dreamless peaceful sleep.

He snatched his dinner off the car's front seat, then snapping his fingers for Belle, he headed around the side of the house.

His bicycle wasn't there.

Of course, it wasn't as if it had a definite parking space against the porch railing. But that was where he thought he'd left it. He supposed somebody could have borrowed it. His sister, Molly, or Marcus or Tommy or one of the other kids might have been at the beach and needed to get somewhere in a hurry. It had happened before. Hugh didn't care. They always brought it back.

But there weren't any tracks in the sand.

There wasn't even any sand.

Someone had swept the walk.

No one *ever* swept the walk. No one but Hugh knew the house even had a stone walkway around the side to the front steps. But as he stared down between his feet, Hugh saw flagstone, not sand, between them.

He rubbed the edge of his flip-flop against it as if it might be a mirage. It was hard, unyielding. He frowned, trying to remember the last time he'd seen the walk.

When he'd bought it, he thought.

Constance, the real estate agent at Island Breeze Property, had taken him to every available house on Pelican Cay, pointing out all the built-ins and the mod cons, the central air and the screened-in porches. He could have had any of them.

He'd wanted a view of the water, a breeze, a place to hang a hammock and no nearby neighbors.

"No indoor plumbing?" Constance had queried.

"That'd be nice." But the truth was, he probably would have bought this place without it. It was exactly what he wanted—old and friendly and undemanding.

But Constance had been unable to stop her rhapsodizing. "It's got ceiling fans in every room, electrical outlets on the porch and a flagstone walk all the way round. So you don' go trackin' in the sand," she'd added in her lovely Bahamian lilt.

Not tracking in sand hadn't been high on Hugh's list of priorities. And he'd never swept it once. Why bother? In five steps he'd be on the beach.

But tonight he was standing on flagstone.

No wonder things felt different. He raised his gaze again to the spot where his bike should have been.

It could have been Molly or Tommy or Marcus. But he somehow doubted it. It wouldn't have occurred to them to sweep the walk before they took it. It wouldn't even have occurred to Lisa Milligan, who probably didn't even realize the walk existed.

It would only have occurred to one person: Sydney St. John.

Hugh laughed aloud, shaking his head. Trust Sydney St. John. Crazy woman.

It wasn't enough to wash every blinkin' dish in the house, she had to sweep his walk before she borrowed his bike to leave. Probably she'd even repaired the hole in the plaster.

Whatever. If she'd taken the bike, she was definitely gone.

He bounded up the steps, whistling—and stopped dead. Not only his bike had gone missing. Everything else had, too.

Well, not everything. The hammock was stirring faintly in the soft breeze. The porch swing was still here. But everything else was—not.

There were no books, no tools, no dirty cups and plates and glasses. No magazines.

Well, actually, yes, there were magazines. In a very neat, perfectly aligned stack, a dozen or so magazines sat on an end table next to the swing.

End table? Hugh raised his brows. He didn't actually remember having an end table. But now that he saw it sitting there uncluttered, it did look vaguely familiar.

Alongside the hammock there was another one. And behind it, a neat row of car parts, plane parts, boat parts and bike parts were all lined up, according to height apparently—with no regard to which vehicle they belonged to—standing at attention.

It was like being back in the Navy again.

A very weird Navy.

Hugh stared. And stared. And then he shifted his gaze slowly and deliberately to some new brick-and-board shelves beneath the window. They held precisely shelved scuba gear. He looked around for his wet suit which usually flapped in the breeze from a plant hook. He wasn't surprised to discover it was no longer there.

He could feel a bellow beginning somewhere in the pit of his stomach. And just as he was about to let it loose, the screen door opened, and there she was—the perpetrator of all this blinking *order!*—Ms. Sydney St. John wearing a sarong and a smile.

Hugh felt as if all the air had been sucked right out of him.

He caught a glimpse or two of the "long, long legs" Maurice had mentioned. And when she moved so did the "real nice curves," which the sarong very thoroughly outlined.

"Ah," she said, beaming. "You're back. Excellent. I thought we might have to eat without you, but—"

He dragged in all the air he could manage. *"Where the hell's my stuff?"*

She waved an arm in an all-encompassing move. "It's straightened up."

"Straightened up? Damn it to hell! What do you think you were doing? How dare you throw my stuff out? Where's my bike? My surfboard? My wet suit? My *life?*"

"In order. For once," she said tartly.

"Order? You call this *order?*" It was like calling Mount Everest a molehill. He expected his spark plugs to stand up and salute!

"Relax. I didn't throw anything away," she said soothingly moving to stand between him and the front door.

It made him instantly suspicious. He stalked across the porch and pushed past her into the house. "God almighty! *What the hell have you done?*"

His life in boot camp hadn't been this organized.

"What you apparently have *never* done. I cleaned house." She followed him in through the living room to the kitchen.

"Who told you—who asked you?" he sputtered, jerking

open cupboards, glowering at the neat stacks of clean dishes. "I told you to do the dishes!"

"I *did* the dishes."

"Yeah. And a whole hell of a lot else," he muttered. The boxes of cereal were organized. So were the canned goods. He thought only obsessive-compulsives alphabetized their spices!

"You can find things now," she told him. "It will be much simpler."

"It was perfectly simple before!" He was furious, well beyond the provocation, and he couldn't even have said why. He wheeled around. "Who told you to do anything?"

"No one had to tell me," she said in an echo of words he'd read in one of those business weeklies he'd read about her today. "I saw what needed to be done and I did it. It's the mark of a good managing director."

His teeth came together with a snap. "I don't *need* a managing director, sweetheart."

Her brows arched. A tiny smile played on the corners of her mouth. "You could have fooled me."

Hugh jammed his fists into the pockets of his shorts and glared. If looks could kill, she'd have been better off eaten by a shark.

She didn't even seem to notice. She simply stood there, smiling, looking cool and competent and mind-shatteringly gorgeous. The sarong was dazzling, in all sorts of rippling blues and greens that brought out the color of her eyes. Tied over one shoulder, it showed far too much of the warm tones of Sydney St. John's skin.

He already had enough memories of her skin. Yesterday at least she'd looked like a boiled lobster. Today, unfairly, the sunburn had turned a dusky gold. She looked delectable. Stunning. Desirable.

And Hugh did not want to desire her. He wanted to throttle her.

"Where's the laundry?" he demanded. "Where are my clothes?"

"Guess," she suggested mildly.

He bared his teeth.

She turned and beckoned him toward the bedroom. He followed warily.

"Amazingly enough," she said, opening drawers and the closet door, "they're put away. The clean ones are all in here. The dirty ones are in the hamper." She nodded toward the wicker basket in the corner. He'd never seen it before. Unlike the end tables, he was sure it was new.

"Where'd that come from?"

"I bought it at the Straw Shoppe."

"Nobody told you to do that, either."

"Consider it a gift."

"You don't have any money."

"I will. I've got a job."

"What?"

She grinned. "I told you I was employable."

"Where? Who hired you?" He'd kill them with his bare hands.

But she just smiled and turned to go back to the kitchen. "I've got to finish getting things ready for dinner."

Dinner?

For the first time he remembered the kitchen table was set for a meal. He turned and strode after her. Damn it to hell, there was even a tablecloth on the table! And place settings for five.

"What the hell is this?" he demanded. "Now what have you done?"

"I invited Molly and Lachlan and Fiona to have dinner with us."

"Molly?" He stared at her. "My *sister* Molly? *And Lachlan and Fiona?* You don't even know Molly and Lachlan and Fiona! Do you?" he demanded, instantly suspicious.

It suddenly occurred to him that his brother knew almost every beautiful woman in the world. And while Lachlan's taste before marriage had run to bimbos, princesses and soccer groupies rather than elegant "managing directors," Hugh doubted he'd have said no to a woman like Sydney St. John.

His teeth came together with a snap.

"Just met them today," Syd replied, unaware that she had just saved his brother's life. "We met this afternoon."

"I told Molly to stay away."

"That's what she said." Syd grinned. "And she minded very well, though I can't understand why."

"She knows what's good for her," Hugh muttered. Molly was a tough cookie, but he and Lachlan had trained her well.

"I ran into her on my way to town. I stopped to admire the *King of the Beach*." Sydney's eyes lit up when she mentioned Fiona's sculpture. "And Molly came out when she saw me there. She told me about it and she introduced herself."

Hugh grunted. That didn't sound too terrible. "So why'd you invite her to dinner?"

"Well, actually she invited me to lunch. Asked me to bring sandwiches back from the bakery when I got finished shopping. So I did. And we talked. About the island. About the sculpture. About Fiona and Lachlan. She told me how it brought them together after them being at odds for years." Syd grinned. "She told me Fiona tipped them into the water and Lachlan followed her to Italy and—"

"God almighty, is there anything she didn't tell you?" Since when had his tough tomboy sister become a giggling gossip?

"She didn't tell me your middle name."

It took him a moment to realize that she was kidding. "I don't pay her to have three-hour lunches," he muttered.

"You don't pay her at all from what I can see. And she was working. So was I. Doing your billing."

He stared at her. "Doing my what? My *billing*? Fly Guy's billing? Who let you—"

"Molly did. She was thrilled. She said she didn't have

time and it needed to be done. She says she hates it—and so do you.''

"I do not!"

"You just defer the pleasure. Whatever. I enjoy it. I think it's fun," she went on blithely. "I love putting numbers in columns. Making things balance. It's orderly."

He just stared at her, unable to think of anything to say. His life wasn't orderly, that was damned sure. She'd knocked it right out of orbit.

"Billing's not difficult," she explained. "Neither's accounting."

"I know that."

"But it helps to have a system." She went on as if he hadn't spoken. "So I started setting up a simple one. I only had a couple of hours today. I had to go clear to Spanish Wells to get plastering compound."

"What?" He stared at her, then turned on his heel and went back into the bedroom. The hole in the wall had been repaired. There was a small patch of still-wet plaster where it had been. He looked at it, shook his head and went back to the kitchen.

"I've never plastered before," Syd said. "I hope it's okay. If it isn't, Lachlan said he knew someone who could do it."

A breath hissed out through Hugh's teeth. "Lachlan? How'd he get involved?"

"He came in while I was setting up the accounting system."

"I don't need you to get a system in place! It's fine the way it is!"

"It's not," she said as if it were simply a matter of fact. *Margaret St. John tells it like it is,* one of the weeklies had proclaimed. Now she said, "It's total chaos. And I'm not the only one who thinks so. Some man named Tom Wilson from someplace called The Lodge called today asking about a bill he didn't get. And a very posh English chap—" her accent became English as she spoke "—Lord

Somebody or Other—Grant Wood? No, that's the painter. He thought so, too.''

"David Grantham," Hugh said heavily.

"Yes, that's him," Syd said happily. "He wanted to know about you flying him to Miami in a few days, and he had some questions about putting together a seaplane excursion for a tour he's doing. But he said he hadn't got a bill from the last one."

"He'll get one," Hugh said through his teeth. "I've been busy."

"That's what I told them. I said you had more than enough to do with all the actual flying and such and that you had discovered that you couldn't possibly deal with the paperwork, as well. But that things had just changed."

Hugh gave her a hard narrow look. "Changed? How?"

"You hired an accountant."

"Like hell!"

"Come on, McGillivray. You need an accountant. Molly needs an accountant. She can't do it all herself."

"No! No way. I didn't hire you!"

"You didn't have to. I did it anyway. Professional courtesy."

"For what? You want me to fly you to Miami? Let's go."

"No. For rescuing me. I owe you. I don't expect you to pay me," she said, her voice intense, her expression serious. "I'm doing it for nothing. It's my way of paying you back."

"I don't need—or want—to be paid back!"

She shrugged. "Well, tough. I need—and want—to do it. You saved my life!"

"My mistake," Hugh muttered, pacing around the kitchen, raking a hand through his hair. But before he could argue further, he heard the sound of footsteps on the porch and Lachlan, Fiona and Molly all trooped in.

"Whoa, look at this!" Lachlan stood, staring around in amazement as if he'd never been in Hugh's house before instead of having spent three months there the spring he moved back to Pelican Cay. His jaw sagged. "I didn't know you had a kitchen."

"Very funny."

"Pretty nifty, huh?" Molly said cheerfully. "Cleans up good, doesn't it? Who'd a thunk it?" She grinned at her brothers.

Fiona stood on the porch, staring at the engine parts. "Look at this. It's almost like one of my sculptures. Really neat rows of junk."

"It's not junk," Hugh said ominously.

Fiona grinned at him "All in the eyes of the beholder. Right, Lach?" She turned her gaze on her husband.

Lachlan nodded. "You must have worked flat out," he said approvingly to Sydney. "All this *and* the stuff at the shop?"

"What about the shop?" Hugh demanded. "What stuff at the shop?"

"All but the old bits and pieces in the back room," Sydney answered Lachlan.

"What old bits and pieces? What back room?" Hugh persisted. "The back room at the shop?"

Molly nodded. "We're organizing. There's way too much stuff. I can never find the parts I need."

"But at least they're there," Hugh argued. "If you clean it out, they'll be gone."

"No, they won't. Not when Fiona's done."

"Fiona? What the hell are you talking about?" How had Fiona got into this?

"Syd had this great idea. Fiona's going to use them in her sculptures," Molly explained. "Like the *King*. Cool, huh? And then if I need a part, Fiona can get it down for me."

"You want to put engine parts on a sculpture?" Had they all lost their minds? "Now just a minute."

But Molly had turned to Fiona. "You *can* get them down if I need them, can't you?"

"Of course."

Hugh tried again to protest, but they talked right over him. The only comment directed his way at all was Lachlan's, "Nice shiner."

Hugh had forgotten about that. He gritted his teeth. "I ran into a door."

"Oh? Syd said it was a wall." Lachlan grinned. "I'm starving. I brought lobsters. Are we going to eat tonight?"

They all turned at once. Fiona set the dozen ears of corn she'd brought onto the counter and began shucking them while Molly put a bowl of peas and rice along with one of potato salad on the table.

Lachlan dumped the passel of spiny lobsters into the kettle of water that Syd had boiling on the back of the stove while Syd, acting as if it were *her* kitchen, quartered and scored pieces of fresh pineapple and set them at each place.

Hugh stood around feeling useless in his own kitchen.

"What's that?" Molly asked, indicating the bag he still held in his hand.

He stared down at it, then remembered. "It's my dinner," he said gruffly. "I didn't realize we were having a party."

"Didn't figure we had to ask," Fiona told him. "I told Syd you were always up for a party."

"We'll go home early," Molly promised him.

Hugh frowned at her. "What? Why?"

His brother looked at him. "Could it be that you're stupider than I thought?"

Fiona kicked Lachlan. "Let him go at his own pace. At least he's going," she hissed.

Hugh looked at them, baffled. "Going?"

"He is," Lachlan mourned. "Completely clueless."

"Hush," Fiona said.

"Time to eat?" Molly suggested hopefully.

They had lobster and salads and all the trimmings. They had key lime pie that Fiona had bought at the bakery for dessert. They drank beer and laughed and talked and included Sydney St. John with a casual acceptance that made Hugh feel as if she had always been there.

One day and she had charmed them all. Had them eating out of her hand.

"Ms. St. John can work with people. She gets the job done," one of the weeklies had proclaimed.

Hugh could see that was true. In one day she knew all about Lachlan's inns and Fiona's sculpture. She had talked to Maurice and Amby, to Sarah at the Straw Shoppe and Erica at the boutique. She knew about the library fund drive and the history museum and the church quilting group. She'd talked to Dave Grantham about his cultural tours and both he and Lachlan had told her about efforts to put together a tourism package.

She even knew about the new clinic that Doc Rasmussen was trying to build and about the fund to buy soccer uniforms for the Pelicans.

Plus she had ideas and suggestions for all of the above. Some of them were a little too big-city, but some of them, Hugh was forced to admit, were surprisingly good.

If she weren't such a pest—arranging and ordering and sorting his house and his shop and his life!—he might have been impressed.

As it was he did his determined best to be indifferent.

It didn't matter how smart and clever and bright and organized—he grimaced—and *gorgeous* Sydney St. John was, he wasn't interested.

She wasn't his kind of woman. She was a Lisa in spades. A forever sort of woman. And one who, no matter what she thought today, wasn't going to stay on Pelican Cay.

"Ms. St. John is going places," one of those weeklies had prophesied.

Hugh absolutely believed it. He just wished she'd hurry up.

She obviously wasn't leaving tonight. So he was stuck

with her that long. But tomorrow, he was flying her to Miami or Nassau or wherever she wanted to go.

"—don't you think, Hugh?"

He jerked back to the present to see Fiona looking at him. They were all sitting in the semidarkness now, with only the glow of his hula girls and flamingos lighting the porch. The soft lazy melody of the new CD of the local steel band played in the background, and obviously Fiona had asked him a question.

"Sorry. I was...distracted."

"I'm sure you are," his sister-in-law grinned. "And probably wishing we'd go home." She stood up, and he could see the outline of her pregnancy in the soft light. "I said I think everything looks wonderful. Put together. Homey. The way I knew this place could be. I think Syd did a great job, don't you?"

"Um..."

"He still misses his old dead batteries and Belle's chewed tennis balls," Lachlan said.

"He'll get over it." Fiona smiled and gave Hugh a look of obvious approval. "I'm so glad. I was worried. I thought you were going to live in never-never land forever."

Never-never land? Hugh sat up straight on the director's chair he'd been lounging back in. Did she think he was bloody Peter Pan just because he didn't fold his laundry and didn't shave every day?

"It's a big improvement, all right," Molly agreed cheerfully before he could ask. She stood up, too, and turned to Hugh. "And you never even said a word!" She punched him lightly on the arm. "I never thought you'd do it. Not after Car— I mean—" She stopped abruptly and took a quick swallow of her beer. "Time I was leaving."

Hugh caught her by the hand. "Pardon me?" he said icily.

Molly tugged free and gave a quick shake of her head. "Nothing. Really. Sorry. I just... I didn't really care what you did, Hugh. If you'd never mar— I mean..." Her voice died once more as she realized that with every word she was getting both feet further and further into her mouth.

In the silence Hugh asked softly, "What is it that doesn't matter if I never do, Mol?"

"Nothing," she said abruptly. "Nothing at all." And she picked up her empty bottle to carry into the kitchen. "Can't leave it here," she said lightly. "There's no clutter."

She disappeared and Fiona and Sydney went after her, carrying more plates and bottles. Lachlan stood and stretched, then slanted Hugh a grin.

"She's dynamite," he said with obvious approval. "Good job."

"She's not—"

"Like all the others," Lachlan said. "Thank God."

Molly and Fiona reappeared. "Thanks for a wonderful evening," Fiona told Hugh, giving him a kiss on the cheek. "And thank you for everything," she said to Sydney.

"I'm so glad you came," Syd said with a smile.

"So are we," Lachlan told her and he gave Syd a kiss. "I'll see you tomorrow."

"Tomorrow?" Hugh scowled.

"Not early," Lachlan promised with a grin. "And it's just business. I'm picking her brain."

"Oh."

Molly laughed. "I love it when you get all territorial." She gave a little laugh, then astonished him by wrapping him in a hug. "I am glad, Hugh," she said fiercely. "You deserve someone wonderful. Enjoy."

And as they all disappeared into the night, Hugh stared after them with the grim realization of what she meant— and that Lachlan and Fiona clearly meant it, too.

Hell. Bloody, bloody hell.

Having Sydney in his house was supposed to convince Lisa Milligan that he was interested in someone else. It wasn't supposed to convince his nearest and dearest that he had a new serious love interest in his life.

Worse, they didn't have to sound so all-fired pleased

about it, as if he were saved at last from the depths of despair and loneliness.

Was that what they had thought ever since Carin had married Nathan Wolfe? Did they imagine that he'd spent the last two years pining away, miserable and forsaken? That he hadn't always shaved or done the dishes because the only woman he'd ever loved had married someone else?

Good God.

And what was he going to do about it?

THE evening had gone surprisingly well.

Much better than Syd imagined it would.

She'd had no doubts, of course, about her ability as a hostess even in unfamiliar circumstances. With a lifetime of practice on behalf of her father and St. John Electronics, she knew how to throw a party for five hundred or an intimate dinner for only a few.

She knew how to be avid, eager and interested. She was a whiz at small talk, capable of making virtually everyone feel at home.

Except the man whose home it actually was.

At least McGillivray had behaved himself. She'd thought he might not.

After the way he had ranted and raved and found fault with everything she had done around the house, she'd expected him to continue in that vein even after his family showed up.

But he hadn't. He'd been quieter than she'd imagined he would be. But after his initial shock, he'd taken part in the conversation. He'd teased his sister and sister-in-law. He'd argued with his brother. And they'd all returned the favor.

Syd had watched and listened, fascinated. And envious. Because, beneath all the jibes, the stories and the teasing, there was such an obvious closeness and affection among them.

She had always wanted siblings. Had wished—had even

suggested—that her father remarry after her mother's death so she could have some.

But that had always been out of the question. Her father had had no interest in remarrying. He'd never even bothered to date anyone seriously after her mother's death. He'd been appalled at her suggestion and had made it quite clear that he had neither the time nor the inclination to invest in another relationship.

And then he'd always put an arm around her and said, "I don't need anyone else. I have you, Margaret."

And she had him.

For her father that had been enough. And Syd had tried to make it—and St. John's—enough for her. But it wasn't. And seeing the McGillivrays together tonight brought that home to her once more.

She wanted what they had. Still, she was a little surprised to be so quickly welcomed and included.

"Your family is so nice," she said to Hugh when they left. She was doing up the last of the dishes, and he was standing with his back to her, staring out the window into the darkness.

When he didn't reply, she went on. "I really enjoyed it."

Still not a word. His shoulders were hunched, his fists shoved into the pockets of his shorts.

"Is the silence your way of saying you didn't enjoy it?" she asked, trying to keep an even, pleasant tone.

The shoulders lifted, but he didn't turn around. "It was fine," he said tonelessly.

There was none of the McGillivray bravado, no quick wit, no sharp reply. She set down the dish towel and moved so she could see his reflection in the window glass. He looked awful.

"What's wrong?" she asked.

He shot her a glare. "Nothing's wrong."

"You're snapping my head off for no reason at all?"

His jaw tightened. Then he consciously seemed to relax

it and flexed his shoulders, which still looked stiff. "It hasn't got anything to do with you." His tone was barely more than a mutter, determinedly dismissive.

But Syd had felt a part of something tonight. And she wasn't going to be dismissed easily. "So, if it's not me, what is it?"

"If I said, 'Mind your own business,' would you?" he asked dryly.

"No."

"It's that Margaret St. John tenacity at work, is it?" He flicked her a sardonic look.

She did a double take. "I thought you didn't know who I was."

"I found out."

"How?"

He shrugged. "While I was waiting for Doc today I was flipping through a couple of magazines."

She named them and he nodded. "So you know I am good at what I do."

"Yep, I know that." His mouth twisted.

"Is that the problem?"

"Of course it's not a problem! Why the hell would it be a problem? You do what you want! It's got nothing to do with me!"

"Then what…?" She was at a complete loss.

McGillivray frowned at her, then raked a hand through his hair. "Didn't you see them tonight? Didn't you hear them? They're just so bloody happy!"

Now it was Syd's turn to frown. "Happy? You mean Molly and Lachlan and Fiona? So what? What's wrong with that?"

"Nothing. Everything! It's what they're happy about!" He looked almost anguished.

Syd stared at him, clueless. "What are they happy about?"

"You. And…me." There was a grim twist to his lips

now. "They're thrilled. They're over the moon at the thought of us…together!"

He made it sound like the end of the world. "Yes. So?"

"That's all you can say?" He gave her an accusing look.

Syd shrugged. "Well, what do you want me to say? What's wrong with that? I thought passing me off as your girlfriend was the whole point. That's what you said."

"To Lisa. Not to them!"

"This is an island," Syd reminded him. "A very little island. How could only Lisa think that? By now everyone on Pelican Cay thinks I'm your girlfriend. Maurice. Amby. Erica. The girl at the Straw Shoppe and the guy at the bakery."

"Jesus!" McGillivray shut his eyes. "Lisa must have shouted it from the rooftops."

"I wouldn't be surprised," Syd said dryly. "Certainly everyone in town knew who I was as soon as I said my name. But," she told him firmly, "you can't blame Lisa for all of it. Molly said you told her."

"Like hell!"

"Well," she amended, "perhaps not in so many words. But she took one look at me and said it was no wonder you wanted her to stay away from the house today."

"You needed to sleep."

"You should have known she'd jump to conclusions."

He groaned. Then he paced the room, cracked his knuckles, muttered under his breath.

Syd watched, trying to fathom it, trying to understand why it mattered so much. Finally she asked, "Is this because of Carin?"

McGillivray's head whipped around and his gaze bored into hers. *"What do you know about Carin?"*

Which answered the question.

"Not much," Syd said quietly, placating him. "Molly just sort of mentioned her and…and you."

"Damn Molly and her jumping to conclusions! I never told her! Never said a word!"

"She's your sister, McGillivray! She's not blind. Obviously, she knows you well enough that you didn't have to say!"

He stared bleakly at her, then dropped into the armchair and leaned back to stare at the ceiling. The sound of the ocean and the lazy whirl of the overhead fan were the only sounds in the room. Syd stood looking at him, wondering if there was anything she ought to say, uncertain what it might be. Finally she just picked up the dish towel again and another plate.

Not until she had finished them all and wiped off the countertop did she come back to where he was sitting. He looked at her, then raked both hands through his hair and dragged his palms down his face.

"Now what?" he said. "What the hell am I supposed to do now?"

"About...Carin?"

"Hell no, not about Carin. That's over! It's past. It never was anything, damn it! We're friends," he said with an ironic twist to the word. "We've *always* been friends. And like a fool I bided my time. Figured she'd come around."

"Molly says—" Syd winced at the look on his face when she once more quoted his sister. But determinedly she pressed forward. "Molly says Nathan is the father of her child."

"So what? I loved Lacey like she was my own."

"I'm sure you did. But maybe Carin never fell out of love with him."

McGillivray dropped his head back against the chair again. He closed his eyes. Syd watched his Adam's apple move as he swallowed.

Then he met her gaze. "She didn't."

Syd nodded slowly. "I'm sorry."

He shrugged and tried for what she was beginning to recognize as his customary determined lightness. "No big deal. Carin's married. She's happy, and I've accepted it."

Had he? Syd wondered.

"The question is, what the hell am I going to do about Molly and Lachlan and Fiona and their bloody assumptions?" he went on, sounding irritable all over again. "That I'm involved? In love?"

He made it sound like a disease. A deadly one.

Syd shrugged. "Don't do anything," she said, irritated herself now, though she couldn't have said exactly why. "Why should you have to *do* anything? Let them think what they think."

"But you'll have to stay awhile."

"So?"

His lips pressed together in a hard thin line.

"You didn't think I was all that distasteful yesterday," she reminded him.

"I didn't do anything about it, either."

Which meant what? That he was going to do something about it now? A nervous thrill shot through her. At the same time she tried to remain cool and calm. "Ms. St. John is unflappable," one of the articles had said.

She could believe her own press when it suited her.

"I'm not marrying you," he said firmly.

Sydney's mouth dropped open. "My God, you're obsessed! What is it with you? Do you see me trying to drag you to the altar!"

He gritted his teeth. "I just want it clear. If you're staying for a while I want you to know where I stand."

"I believe I've figured it out," Syd said icily.

He gave a quick jerky nod. "Fine. Then when we've convinced them that I'm not pining away for Carin, we can break it off and you can leave."

"We can break it off," Syd agreed. "But I'm not leaving."

"Yes, you are." His tone brooked no argument, but Syd ignored it.

"I can stay if I want. We can both—"

"No." He stood up, looking suddenly fierce and powerful. "We can't both. It doesn't work that way. The island is too small. You *saw* how small it was today. Everyone knows everything. There are no lies on Pelican Cay. Not ones that survive more than a couple of weeks, anyway.''

"But—"

"We can get away with it that long. Then it's over. We're finished. We break up. You go away.''

"I can—"

"You can't," he said without letting her finish. "You're not going to want to stay, anyway,'' he informed her flatly. "You're a woman on the move, remember? You just want to make Roland Whatsit pay.''

Syd would have argued with him, but there was no point.

Of course she wanted Roland to sweat. But she wanted more than that. And it had nothing to do with moving and everything to do with figuring out who she was and becoming her own person at last.

When she'd told McGillivray last night that she intended to find a job here, she'd been blue-skying, throwing out an idea, listening to it echo, testing it against reality.

The clear light of day hadn't changed her mind. In fact, everything she'd seen and done today on Pelican Cay had confirmed it.

She liked the island and everything about it. She liked the soft sand beach, the turquoise water, the jumble of pastel stucco and clapboard houses. She liked the narrow roads and raised wooden sidewalks and the quaint shops that edged the palm-lined quay. She liked the friendly people. There was none of the anonymity she'd grown up with. Everyone knew their neighbors, for good or for ill.

Everyone knew McGillivray. And obviously everyone— not just his sister and his brother and his sister-in-law— cared about him. They'd all said so, in one way or another—Tony at the bakery, Stella at the Cotton Shoppe, the old lady Miss Saffron on her porch when Syd had passed.

All of them, one way or another, had said, "So you're McGillivray's girl? He's a good man. You be good to him.''

It had made her think differently about McGillivray. But more than that, it had made her want someone to care about her that way.

"We'll take things one day at time," she said.

"And when it's over, you'll leave." It wasn't a question. Blue eyes bored into hers.

Syd sighed softly. "When the time comes, I'll leave."

McGillivray's gaze narrowed. "When the time comes? What's that mean?"

"It means that I'm sure we'll both know when." And it left things open-ended and vague.

McGillivray looked as if he might argue. But finally he let out a slow deep breath. For a long moment neither spoke. Their eyes met. Their gazes locked.

The sizzle was there again. Still. It didn't surprise Syd as much this time. What surprised her was that something else was there, too. Something deeper and even more compelling.

A memory flickered through her mind of what McGillivray had looked like with his eyes closed and his lips parted. She remembered what the hard warmth of his body had felt like, and how solid his arm had felt wrapped across her.

She saw him swallow and wondered what he was remembering.

"I hope to hell," he said raggedly, "that while you were turning this place into 'house beautiful' today, you moved into the spare room."

CHAPTER SIX

SYD was in the spare room.

Hugh was alone in his. Theoretically.

In fact, memories of her kept intruding. He lay awake long after he should have fallen asleep—thinking, muttering, tossing and turning.

But he didn't just think about Syd. He thought about a lot of things. About life—about goals, purpose, focus, meaning. All the deep and significant issues that, in the course of day-to-day living, Hugh pretty much pretended didn't matter.

He had, after all, built his image on that foundation.

Ever since he'd come along, the second son in a family where the first son had already decided he was Going-To-Be-the-Best, Hugh had committed himself to doing the opposite. Mr. Laid-Back, Easy-Come-Easy-Go, Nothing-Much-Matters - but - a - Cold - Beer - and - a - Long - Nap McGillivray, that was him.

On the surface at least.

Deep down in a place he acknowledged to no one but himself, Hugh knew he had as many goals as his brother. For one, he'd made up his mind to find work that would let him come back to Pelican Cay. And he'd done it. He'd figured out what would work on the island, what he'd like doing, and he'd mastered the skills to make it pay. If it looked like he was loafing half the time, so be it. He liked to loaf, too.

He'd done the same thing when he'd bought his house.

It was all the things Constance had told him it was, but it was also, he'd figured, a good place to start a family.

Hugh had always wanted a family. Lachlan had been the jet-setter. Molly had been the loner, eager to see the world.

Hugh liked to fly, enjoyed going places, but even more he liked coming home. He liked *being* home.

He'd always figured by now he'd be the easy-going family man, settled down with a wife and kids. When he'd met Carin and her daughter, Lacey, he'd simply figured they'd have a head start on the kids.

Right from the start, though, when he'd come back to the island and met her for the first time, he'd known he would have to go slow with her. She'd been hurt, Maurice had told him. She didn't need hurting again.

Hugh knew he would never hurt her. He never had. He'd always been her friend. He'd been Lacey's friend. He'd loved being their friend. He still did. But he'd always wanted more and he'd believed someday Carin would return the feelings he was careful to keep hidden for fear of spooking her. When the time was right, he'd assured himself, she would forget the man who had hurt her and marry the man who loved her.

He never in a million years figured Nathan would come back and make Carin fall in love with him all over again. But he had. And the rest was history.

The trouble was, Hugh admitted for the first time, he still wanted what he'd wanted with her. He wanted a home, a wife, a family.

He'd been playing the field for two long years. Lisa had put a stop to it recently by her persistence, and he'd convinced himself he needed a buffer against her so he could start playing the field again.

But it wasn't true. The truth was he wanted exactly what Lisa Milligan wanted—marriage, a home, a family. Only not with her.

Then who?

And of course that was when the images of Sydney St. John started playing over again in his head.

It was pointless. Futile. Useless. She was gorgeous and there was definitely a spark between them. He felt it at least. But he'd thought he felt it with Carin, and God knew she hadn't.

How much less likely to was the perfect professional Ms. St. John?

It didn't even bear thinking about.

Sydney St. John wasn't going to stay around Pelican Cay. She was, as both the articles he'd read had pointed out, a woman on the move. She was "going places."

She was here now. This minute. And maybe for the next two weeks. Long enough to help him convince his concerned family that he was well and truly over Carin and getting on with his life.

But then she would be gone.

And someday he would read another article about her society wedding. He had no doubt she would marry. He'd listened to her this evening talking eagerly and a little enviously to his sister-in-law about the baby Fiona was expecting.

"It must be the most amazing experience," Syd had said, smiling and placing a hand reverently on Fiona's slightly rounded belly.

"If you like throwing up every morning and feeling wrung out by two in the afternoon," Fiona had replied in her flat no-nonsense way. But she had smiled a conspiratorial smile at her husband as she said it.

And Syd had not been deterred. "It's worth it," she'd said.

Fiona, meeting Lachlan's eyes with a smile, agreed, "Yes, it is."

So someday, then, Syd would be somebody's mother. Some little up-and-coming CEO who would follow in Mommy and Daddy's footsteps. She might not marry old Roland Whosits, but Hugh had no doubt there would be a less inept CEO who would come along and sweep her off her feet, a man whose goals and lifestyle echoed hers.

Not some backwater bush pilot like him.

They would be playing house for a couple of weeks so she could make Carruthers sweat and he could convince his family that he'd moved on with his life.

And then she would go.

That settled, Hugh yawned and rolled over. He wrapped his arms around his pillow and hauled it hard against him. It wasn't nearly as satisfying as having his arms around Sydney St. John.

But it was a whole lot smarter.

If she had another nightmare he could go in and see if she was all right, though.

He listened intently for sounds of nightmares. But other than the sea and the fan and Belle's soft snoring, he heard nothing.

Just as well.

He was finally drifting off to sleep when he remembered she'd never told him what job she'd supposedly got. He was tempted to get up and go to her room and ask her. Sanity prevailed.

He'd ask her in the morning.

But when he got up in the morning, she was gone.

"WHERE the hell have you been? Don't you know better than to go swimming alone?"

Syd looked at the man blocking her way on the path back to the house, his hair uncombed, his face unshaven, wearing only a pair of shorts that rode low on lean hips, and she swallowed the surge of pure female appreciation of the male of the species and smiled brightly. "And a very good morning to you, too."

McGillivray grunted. "You shouldn't swim alone," he repeated.

"Then come with me tomorrow. It's glorious out there. I can't believe how warm the water is." She kept smiling at him, even though he didn't move and was still frowning. "Are we going to stand here all day or are you going to let me past?"

Grudgingly he stepped aside, and she nipped past him, wishing as she did so that she dared reach out and touch the muscular chest or press a kiss to the thin, hard line of his lips. The electricity she felt every time she saw him showed no signs of abating. On the contrary, it seemed especially strong this morning.

She turned to look back. "Do you ever swim in the morning?"

"Sometimes." He was following her back to the house, but taking his time, not catching up.

"Alone?" she asked innocently, with a light of laughter in her voice as his brows drew down. "I wasn't alone the whole time," she told him. "I ran into some boys playing soccer. Doing drills, they said, like Lachlan taught them. And then they came swimming with me. They told me there's a wreck out beyond the reef. A really old ship, they said, with cannons." It sounded marvelous.

McGillivray nodded. "Yeah. It was wrecked about three hundred years ago during a storm. It was supposed to be coming through the narrows and got washed up against the reef."

She climbed the steps, then turned to wait for him. "Have you ever seen it?"

"Of course. Everybody's seen it."

"I haven't. I've never seen a sunken ship before." She looked past him toward the ocean in the distance. "The reef's not that far," she said speculatively.

"Too far to swim," McGillivray said flatly, "and way too dangerous."

"Dangerous?" Syd frowned. "Why?"

"Remember your friend, the shark?" A grin slashed across his face.

"But you said everybody went."

"In boats. And they don't go alone."

"Fine. Maybe Tommy and Lorenzo could take me. They were two of the boys playing soccer," she explained.

"I know who they are. Tommy is Fiona's nephew."

"Oh. Right. Small island. Everyone knows everyone else. I keep forgetting. Sorry." She felt foolish then and turned to hurry into the house.

"I could take you," McGillivray said.

She spun around. "Really? You wouldn't mind?"

He shrugged. "Why not? Probably be a good idea," he said gruffly. "Since we're a 'couple.'" His mouth twisted as he said the last word.

Syd's joy faded a little at his attitude. But not much. She was having too good a morning to let him ruin it with his grouchiness. She nodded. "Yes," she agreed. "Then we could tell everyone we'd done it. Together."

"We won't have to tell anyone," McGillivray said with grim certainty. "They'll know."

HE WAS, Syd discovered, absolutely right.

An hour later, when she was walking into town to start her job, Miss Saffron hailed her as she passed. "I hear you goin' to be workin' for Erica," she called.

Syd smiled at the other woman's question. "That's right."

"You good at all them numbers?" Miss Saffron asked.

"Yes."

"Maybe you talk to my nephew, Otis, at the hardware store. He need somebody who do numbers. On a computer, yes?"

"Yes. I'll talk to him," Syd promised.

Miss Saffron smiled. "Good. So, when you an' Hugh goin' out to see that ol' wreck?"

Now Syd stared in astonishment. "How did you know we talked about the wreck?" she demanded. She'd left Hugh eating breakfast at the house an hour ago. She was sure he hadn't picked up the phone and called Miss

Saffron to tell her anything of the sort. He seemed to think the islanders knew far too much already.

Miss Saffron shrugged ample shoulders. "Just makes sense. Lorenzo say he tell you 'bout it this mornin. Say he take you." She grinned broadly, then shook her head. "But I tell him, no chance. Ain't nobody takin' you nowhere but our Hugh."

And Syd smiled, nodding slowly. "Right," she murmured. "That's right."

"Hurry on now. Erica be waitin'."

Dismissed, Syd gave Miss Saffron a wave as she started once more down the hill. On the corner she passed the hardware store. Otis was sweeping the sidewalk out front.

"Hey, there, Hugh's girl," he called to her, "wouldn't mind talkin' to you."

HUGH'S girl.

That's what they were calling her. Everywhere he went that morning, he heard about his new girlfriend.

"Hugh's girl," Amby said. "She's pretty as a sunset."

"Hugh's girl," Otis said, "is smart as a whip."

"Hugh's girl—" everybody made sure they told him "—is just about perfect."

Hugh wasn't surprised. And he didn't protest. It was, after all, what he wanted them all to think.

But all the same, it was getting under his skin.

He was glad they liked her, of course. He liked her. Too damn much. He didn't want everybody else thinking she was wonderful, too. Then, when she left, they'd really be thinking he was a loser.

Hell. Oh, hell.

Which was why he strode into Lachlan's office at the Moonstone that afternoon.

"Hey, there." Lachlan looked up from his desk and grinned. "I like your girlfriend."

"You and the whole damn world."

Lachlan blinked. He tipped back in his chair and regarded his brother curiously. "That's a bad thing?"

"Of course not." Hugh cracked his knuckles, prowled the room, craned his neck to look out the window to see who was walking along the beach.

"She's got a lot of really good ideas about island development," Lachlan said.

"She could run it with one hand tied behind her back," Hugh agreed grimly.

Lachlan grinned. "Maybe we should elect her mayor."

"Like hell!"

"Want to keep her home all for yourself?"

"No! Yes! Oh, cripes. I don't know why I even came over here."

"Neither do I," Lachlan said. "But it's always a pleasure," he added piously, still grinning.

"Shut up." Hugh did another lap of the office.

Lachlan, watching him, shook his head. "You've got it bad, don't you?" He sounded cheerful.

"Got what?"

His brother rolled his eyes. "That's right, deny it. Is she giving you trouble?" he asked almost sympathetically.

Hugh slowed his pacing and shrugged. "It's not that," he said. But he couldn't exactly say what it was, either.

"Where'd you meet her?"

"I fished her out of the drink."

Lachlan laughed. "Whatever works."

"I'm not kidding!"

Lachlan tipped his chair forward again. "Did I say you were?" Blue eyes exactly the same color as his own stared back at Hugh. "When a guy finds the right woman, he does whatever he's gotta do."

Hugh snorted. "Like you had to do anything to get Fiona." She'd been sitting here waiting for Lachlan for years, and other than her brief stint in Italy she hadn't any intention of going anywhere.

"You'd be surprised," Lachlan said dryly over steepled fingers.

Hugh's eyes widened. "I would," he agreed. "Tell all."

Lachlan shook his head. "Not on your life. I got my woman. That's all I'm going to say." He met Hugh's eyes again. "Except that it's worth it, and I'll do whatever I can to help you keep yours."

"I don't have her yet," Hugh said. "It might not work out."

Lachlan scowled. "Why the hell not?"

Hugh shrugged. "We have to both want the same thing. We might not." He might as well lay the groundwork for when she would leave.

"Don't be stupid," Lachlan protested. "You're the best guy in the world—besides me." He grinned.

Hugh grinned back, but his heart wasn't in it. "Even so. It might not work out. I'm staying here. It's a given. She might not. I can't force it. And neither can you," he warned his brother, who was likely to try.

"But she says she wants to," Lachlan argued.

"Now," Hugh agreed. "Who's to say how she'll feel a ways down the road."

SHE felt more and more at home.

As the days passed, she settled in. She worked at Erica's two mornings a week, at Otis's one. She spent the other mornings helping Molly at Hugh's shop doing the accounting and the billing.

"It's a waste of your talent," McGillivray told her.

"But it makes me happy," she told him.

He wasn't convinced, but other than rearranging the cells in his brain, she didn't see how she could convince him. She did think that he realized she liked other parts of life on Pelican Cay.

He'd taken her out to see the wreck one afternoon. He'd begun the expedition in his usual grumpy fashion, but he'd responded to her determined questions, and he'd been patience personified when he'd taught her to snorkel. And after, when she'd told him it was one of the best days of her life, he'd actually looked pleased before he'd shrugged and turned away.

That had been a letdown. But Syd was accustomed to disinterest. Her father had been a past master at it. His, she'd learned long ago, was the real thing.

McGillivray's wasn't.

It was *studied* disinterest. *Determined* disinterest.

How did she know?

Because sometimes when he thought she wasn't looking, she caught him watching her, studying her almost. And when she turned then and spoke to him, he would quickly look away.

Why?

He liked women. They'd established that the first evening. He liked her. On a purely physical level he'd been attracted to her right from the start. They'd established that, too. And though he liked to pretend she annoyed him even now, she dared to think he actually enjoyed her company.

If he didn't, why was he getting up to go swimming with her in the mornings now? And why did he let her come along when he walked Belle on the beach at night? And why did he sit around in the evenings and talk to her? He knew more about the history of Pelican Cay than anyone on the island, she was sure of it. She'd asked a lot of people a lot of questions. No one knew more than Hugh.

At first he stopped himself whenever he began to talk about the early days, saying, "It doesn't matter. You wouldn't be interested."

But if she persisted and asked questions, he always answered. She could always get him talking again, telling her about the island's past, its pirates and its politicians, its rascals and its rogues, the swashbuckling seafarers who had long ago called Pelican Cay home. The island and its stories were in his blood, she could tell.

And as the days passed, the island and its stories—and Hugh McGillivray—were in hers.

She felt a connection to him she'd never felt to any other man. It was electric and it was sexual, no doubt about that. She hadn't even had to have made love with him to know that. But it was also something more.

He was a kindred spirit. She sensed it. He was a friend— when he wasn't trying to deny it.

He could be her soul mate. And there was a mind-boggling thought. But it was true—all the things she'd always wanted in a man and had begun to think she'd never find, she was discovering in Hugh McGillivray.

But McGillivray was keeping her at a distance.

Why?

Because he didn't trust her. That much she understood at once. He knew who she was, where she had come from—and he didn't trust that she would stick around. He didn't trust that her mornings as an accountant-bookkeeper would satisfy her.

And in the long run, he was probably right.

Well, fine. The jobs had been a stopgap measure, a means of paying her way, of making sure she was self-sufficient. She could do more. Right here on the island she could do more. She was sure of it.

She'd learned a lot from Hugh about the island's history. She'd learned a lot from the islanders about its assets. She'd also learned from her earlier work how to make the best of what she was given. She'd tossed out some ideas to Lachlan that first evening. They had come off the top of her head. Now she had more.

She picked up the phone and called him. "Lachlan? Sydney, here. I've been thinking. I have something I'd like to talk to you about. I wonder if you'd have time to see me tomorrow morning."

"How about lunch?" he suggested. "At Beaches? Dave Grantham came in this afternoon. He said he'd talked to you once on the phone. I know he'd like to meet you again.''

"Sounds great. I'll meet you there.''

She hung up, pleased. One step toward her future had been accomplished. Tomorrow she would take the second.

But first she had the past to deal with.

"HI, DAD. It's Sydney,'' Syd said into the phone. "I just wanted to tell you I'm resigning.'' Her voice sounded firm and resolute and she was glad. It was the first time she'd ever told her father something he didn't want to hear.

"Sydney?'' Simon St. John sounded momentarily mystified. "Oh, Margaret,'' he corrected her. "Good to hear from you. And of course you're resigning,'' he went on cheerfully. "I told Roland you wouldn't want to continue working after you were married.''

So he *had* known. She'd always held out hope that the idea had been Roland's alone. Now she felt a hollow ache in her midsection. But it didn't hurt the way it would have a week before. It simply stiffened her resolve.

"I'm not married, Dad,'' she said calmly.

There was a moment's stunned silence.

Then, "What? Not married? What do you mean? Roland said you and he were getting married after the merger. Two mergers, he said.'' Simon's voice went from pleased as he reported Roland's witticism to perplexed as he tried to reconcile Syd's denial of it. "What happened? Why not? Don't tell me you're dithering? You were never the dithering sort, Margaret.''

"I'm not the dithering sort now, Dad. I didn't marry Roland because I didn't want to.''

"But he said you would!''

"He was mistaken.''

"Put him on the phone,'' Simon demanded. "I want to talk to him. Now.''

"I'm sorry. He's not here.''

"What do you mean not there? Where are you, Margaret?"

"I'm in the Bahamas. I don't know where Roland is. But I just called to tell you I'm staying. I don't expect you to understand. But this is something I have to do."

"Staying? For how long? For heaven's sake, Margaret! Have you lost your mind?"

"No. I think I finally found it," Syd said, and knew the truth of the words she spoke.

"Have you had an accident? Have you fallen and hit your head?"

"No, Dad. I haven't fallen. I'm fine. In fact, I've never been better."

"Then, I don't understand." He sounded almost petulant now. "Why isn't Roland with you? What's going on? I thought you were on your honeymoon!"

"No honeymoon. No Roland. I have to go, Dad. I just wanted you to know I'm fine. Tell Roland 'thank you' when he calls. I'll be in touch."

"Tell Roland 'thank you'?" His voice was rising. "For what? Now you listen to me, Margaret—"

But Syd had listened to him far too long already. "Bye, Dad. I love you."

And she hung up.

"YOU'RE what?" Hugh stared at Syd when she met him at the door of the kitchen, a bottle of champagne in her hand. He shook his head, certain he hadn't heard her right.

"I'm the new coordinator of the Pelican Cay Development Organization," she repeated, which was more or less what he thought she'd said the first time. She was beaming and waving the champagne.

"Coordinator of the Pelican Cay Development Organization? What the bloody hell is that?"

He'd been counting the days until he could tell her their charade was over, that she could pack her bags and head for the big city and bright lights, certain that she'd be happy to leave him and the island and her humdrum accounting jobs.

And now she was *what?*

"It's a new position," she admitted. "Just formed. Just funded actually. But it's real."

"Says who?"

"Your brother, for one. And Lord Grantham. Lachlan and David and I had lunch today."

He might have known! Damn his meddling, interfering brother anyway!

"The organization exists. You must know that."

"They hold bake sales," Hugh said scathingly. "And they sell used paperbacks for the library."

"Well, now they're doing more than that," Syd said stiffly. "It doesn't pay much yet. But that's okay because I can live on savings for a while. I will get a basic salary. Enough to live on. But it's a place to start. To develop. To make a commitment," she said, looking straight at him. "And when things get rolling, it will be terrific."

Bloody hell. Hugh pushed past her into the kitchen. She'd set the table with a tablecloth and candles. Like some damned celebration!

Syd followed him in. "We're going to put Pelican Cay on the map," she told him. "We're going to develop the tourism industry, target suitable U.S. and European markets, manage growth, involve the entire community and make sure that the island thrives without being overwhelmed."

Hugh stared at her. "We are? Or *you* are?"

"All of us," she said firmly, meeting his gaze. She ran her tongue over her lips. He couldn't help noticing them even though he jerked his gaze away. "I'm the facilitator," she continued. "That means I smooth the way." She explained the term as if he was a grade-school kid.

"I know what it means," Hugh told her through his teeth. "You said you would leave."

"I said we would both know when it was right," she corrected.

"It's right," he told her. He'd been living in some sort of fool's paradise all week. Spending time with her, going swimming with her, taking walks with her, talking for hours with her. Pretending they were a couple! And it was killing him.

He ground his teeth. "When you and I split, you said you'd leave. You agreed."

"We haven't split."

"We will."

"We don't have to."

"We damned well do!"

"Why? We can make it work," she told him, "as long as we think ahead. As long as we account for all the possibilities and factor everything in."

"Oh, really?" Hugh said savagely. "What about *this* possibility? Have you factored in *this?*"

He took three swift steps across the kitchen, snatched the spoon from her hand and dropped it on the counter, then hauled her hard against him and kissed her!

The kiss was fierce, furious, frustrated. In it was all the desire and yearning he'd ever felt for the woman who would someday share his hopes and his dreams and his joys, his very life. In it there was all the pent-up need and emotion and desperation he'd felt for days.

Days, hell! Months! Years!

If only…

And then, dear God, he wasn't just kissing Sydney St. John.

She was kissing him back!

Her mouth was open, her tongue was tangling with his. The soft curves of her body were pressed against the hard planes of his own. The bottle slipped unnoticed from her hand, fell on the floor and rolled, and her fingers tangled in his hair. His arms wrapped around her, drew her even more tightly against him. His hips surged with a need he'd denied far too long.

"Yesss."

He heard the word hiss through her lips, felt her hands slide between them to press against his chest. But not to resist. Not to hold him off. To touch, to stroke, to incite.

He jerked back while he still had a sane cell in his brain. His chest was heaving. His heart pounded like the propellers right before takeoff. He stared at her, aching, needing. Wanting.

And furious as hell that *she* wanted, too!

CHAPTER SEVEN

HUGH flung shirts and shorts, underwear and socks—everything he'd need for a couple of days away—into his duffel bag. Not that a couple of days was going to solve the problem.

Nothing would solve the problem short of Sydney St. John flying away and never coming back. But she wasn't doing that. She was waltzing around the house like they hadn't nearly burned it down last night!

No thanks to her that they hadn't.

Cripes, he could still taste her now, could still remember the way her mouth had opened to him, the way she'd drawn him closer, pressed harder, urged him on.

He jerked open another drawer and dumped half the contents into his bag. God knew if he would need any of it. He just needed to get away.

He sent up a prayer of thanksgiving for Tom Wilson's stopping him on his way into The Grouper last night, saying he had business in Miami beginning tomorrow and wondering if Hugh might be able to take him.

"If you can take me on from there, too," he'd said, "that'd be fantastic. If not, I can hire a pilot once I get to Miami."

"I can do it," Hugh had said. If it hadn't been already dark he'd have suggested they leave right then.

Instead he told Tom he'd meet him at the dock at nine, then he'd shouldered his way into The Grouper determined to drown his desire in a bottle of whiskey.

It would be all over the island in minutes, he knew.

"Hugh's in The Grouper. *Alone!*"

The buzz had begun almost as soon as he'd come through the door. He ignored it. So what if they muttered and tittered and gossiped that he and Syd were having problems?

By God, they *were* having problems.

If lusting after the most unsuitable woman in the world wasn't a problem, he didn't know what was. And having her welcome his advances was an even bigger disaster!

What the hell had she been thinking?

Well, obviously she hadn't. So he was going to have to think for both of them.

Something about the purposeful way he'd strode in and demanded whiskey must have made things clear. Michael the bartender wordlessly handed him a bottle and a glass and nodded his head toward a small table in the back.

Hugh took it, then sat with his back to the wall, hunched over his glass, glaring at anyone who showed the slightest sign of coming near.

Only one person had. Lisa Milligan came in with a couple of girlfriends, saw him by himself and her face lit up.

Bloody hell.

"Hugh. Haven't seen you around lately," she said smiling as she stopped at his table. "Did your friend leave?"

"No." He set his glass down with a thump, then poured himself another.

"I, um, see."

He doubted it very much.

She didn't leave, though. Instead she cocked her head and asked sympathetically, "Is something wrong?"

"What do you think?" he snarled, sick and tired of being Mr. Nice Guy, careful of everyone else's feelings. Look where the hell that had got him. And what about his own feelings for a change?

Lisa shifted from one foot to the other nervously. "Would you like to, um, join us?" she asked after a moment, her tone falsely cheerful. But she seemed so worried and so helpless that Hugh couldn't bite her head off, even though he wanted to.

"No. Thanks." He took a deep breath and sighed, then added more whiskey to his glass and downed the whole thing before looking up at her. "You're a sweet girl, Lisa, but I don't want any company tonight." Or ever.

Which was probably what he should have said a long time past.

Lisa smiled wanly. She nodded. "Of course." She backed away, still smiling her nervous smile. "Maybe another time, then?"

Hugh stared into his whiskey glass. "Yeah, Lisa. Maybe another time."

After Lisa, no one else came near. Lots of people looked his way, murmured to each other, sighed and shook their heads, then moved on. They ought to know in Nassau tomorrow that he and Syd had broken up.

Who gave a damn? Hugh thought viciously, downing another shot and slapping the glass on the table. They'd never been together in the first place.

He'd just wanted—

He poured another whiskey and stared at the liquid swirling in the glass. He studied it in the dim light. Lifted it. Tasted it. Swallowed it. It burned like the others had. It didn't seem to be deadening anything—least of all the memory of the taste of Sydney St. John's mouth.

He didn't pay any attention to the passage of time. There was no point. He wasn't going home until he had to.

All the same, well before he was ready he heard, "Closin' time, mon," and looked up to see Michael standing beside the table, his windbreaker on, the keys to lock up in his hand.

There was nothing left in the bottle, anyway. Hugh nodded and hauled himself to his feet. The room reeled lazily, dipped and swayed.

"You okay?" Michael asked.

"Just swell," Hugh lied. "Never better." He spotted the

door and aimed toward it. It kept moving. Stools got in the way.

Michael's hand settled on his shoulder and steered him around them, then outside onto the steps. "You drink the whole thing?"

"Yep."

"Lotta whiskey." Michael shook his head. "Can you make it home?"

"Eventually."

"I can call a taxi. My dad'll give you a lift."

Hugh tried to shake his head. "I'll walk. 'S a nice night."

"Storm brewin', so they say." Michael studied the stars. "Blow through in a coupla days."

Storm had been here already to Hugh's way of thinking. He shrugged. "Long as it lets me go. I'm flying out in the morning. Goin' to Miami."

"With your lady?"

"No!" Hugh's ferocity surprised even himself. He rubbed his hands down his face, then said it again more quietly. "No."

Michael patted his shoulder. "Like that, is it?"

"Like what?" Hugh scowled.

White teeth flashed in the darkness. "Can't live with 'em. Can't live without 'em."

Wasn't that the truth, Hugh thought as he walked slowly home.

And this morning he had the hangover to prove it.

His head pounded. His mouth tasted like the bottom of a tide pool. His eyes felt as if they had barnacles under the lids. And he wished to God Syd would stop banging pots and pans while she sang in the kitchen. How the hell much noise did a woman have to make?

He rolled up a pair of khakis and tossed them into the bag, then threw in his loafers on top of them. Maybe he'd go out tonight. Live it up a little. Meet a gorgeous woman to take his mind off the gorgeous woman driving him crazy.

He zipped up the bag and walked out into the kitchen. Syd had her back to him, still singing cheerfully, rubbing his face in his pain.

"I'm going to Miami," he said harshly.

She turned around. Her gaze flicked from his face to the duffel in his hand, but she didn't say anything, just looked at him.

"I could give you a ride," he offered. One more chance. *Say you're leaving like you promised.* "Get you back to your real life."

She shook her head. Slowly. Adamantly. "This is my real life. I resigned my job."

The last thing he wanted to hear.

He shrugged. "Suit yourself. And find yourself a place to move to while I'm gone."

Something—hurt?—flickered in her gaze. She pressed her lips together. "I'll do that," she said stiffly.

"I'm staying over," he told her, his tone flat and abrupt. "Don't know how long I'll be gone. I can't take Belle. Do you want her here? If not, she can go to Molly's."

"I'll keep her."

They stared at each other. Seconds passed.

"You can leave anytime," Hugh told her. "If you change your mind, just drop her with Molly."

"I told you I'm staying. I'm not going to leave."

Their gazes locked. Hugh's slid away first. He found himself staring at her mouth, found himself wanting to kiss her again.

"Oh, hell," he muttered. "I'm outta here."

SYD stared at the lists on the table.

Lists of contacts, of artists, artisans and craftspeople. Lists of island attractions and accommodations, of restaurants and motorbike rentals, of fishing guides for hire and scuba diving gear.

"All the possibilities," she'd told Lachlan and David

yesterday, waving the lists at them. "I always think of all the possibilities."

But it wasn't true.

Not when it mattered. Not when it came to herself.

Just like when Roland had announced their impending marriage, she'd missed something vital.

Not anymore, she decided. Like Sleeping Beauty, kissed out of her slumber, Hugh's kiss had awakened her to a new reality—and all sorts of possibilities she hadn't dared think about.

But now she did.

Last night she had responded instinctively, eagerly, desperately. She had wanted Hugh McGillivray as she'd never wanted anyone in her life. She'd wanted his kiss, his body.

Love?

"Love?" She said the word aloud, tasting it, testing it. She sat still, staring into space. And then, because she was Sydney St. John, who had grown up making plans and drawing up lists, she printed the word out one letter at a time: *L.O.V.E.* on a piece of paper and stared at it.

"Love?" she said in barely a whisper this time. "I love him."

The knowledge was deep and profound and so very basic that it took her by surprise. It wasn't like a business plan or a merger or anything else that you had to think about beforehand and study all the angles of. It had simply happened.

"I love him," she said again, testing the words once more. He was completely wrong for her. Too hard, too sloppy, too opinionated, too stubborn.

And yet...

"I love him," she said.

Belle's tail thumped.

So did Syd's heart. She took a quick tremulous breath, realized she was strangling the pen in a death grip and consciously made her fingers loosen and relax. Instead they shook.

A kaleidoscope of McGillivray impressions formed and reformed in her mind—McGillivray playing with Belle, McGillivray running on the beach, McGillivray teaching her to snorkel, McGillivray telling her about some esoteric bit of island lore. McGillivray in bed with his arm around her. McGillivray's lips on hers. McGillivray's tongue tangling with hers.

Oh, heavens. Oh, dear. Oh, help.

Oh, yes.

The question was: What was she going to do about it?

Because even as she recognized her feelings for what they were—considerably more than simple lust—at the same time she had to acknowledge that he certainly wasn't in love with her.

She'd thought when she'd taken the job Lachlan and David had offered that doing so would prove to Hugh that she would stay, and that then he would trust her, and might be willing to explore "possibilities" with her.

Now she wanted more than possibilities.

She wanted his love.

And he loved Carin Campbell. Carin was—he'd never denied it—the woman he'd hoped to spend his life with. And even though he couldn't—and had accepted it—that didn't mean he wanted second best.

He had kissed her. He had wanted her. But it had been nothing more than pure physical hunger. Urgent hunger, to be sure. But urgency wasn't love.

All it meant was that he was a male living in close proximity with a female he found sexually appealing.

Nothing else.

Yet.

Time stopped.

Syd did, too. She stared at the word *love* on the paper in front of her. She knew the truth of it for her. But not for Hugh.

He wasn't in love with her *yet*.

Syd drew a slow, careful, apprehensive breath. Was it

possible for Hugh McGillivray's feelings to change? Could urgent physical attraction turn into something more? Something deeper? Something lasting?

It had for her.

The simple realization jolted her, made her heart kick over, made the next breath she took come in a fast gulp. Her feelings for him had changed completely since she'd first met him. Why, then, couldn't his change as well?

"They could," she breathed.

"They *can*," she said more firmly. She ventured a smile, then dared a grin. "Think of it as a challenge," she whispered to herself. Because God knew it was. A far bigger challenge than organizing the assets and opportunities for tourism on Pelican Cay.

But Syd relished a challenge. She thrived on them. She didn't know how to change a man's mind. She didn't know how to alter his feelings.

She only knew she had to try.

"You never know until you try," her father always said.

Simon St. John had made his fortune trying and succeeding at things that other people hadn't thought were possible. He'd also had some colossal failures, Syd reminded herself. He had not been a notably good father, in fact.

But he'd made the effort. He'd done his best in his limited way. And that was better, she had to admit, than not trying.

Heaven help her, she was apparently Simon's daughter after all.

TUESDAY passed and Hugh didn't come back.

Syd prowled the waterfront most of the day, ostensibly creating a map of Pelican Town with "points of interest" for visitors, but all the while watching for signs of his seaplane. It never came.

He didn't come back on Wednesday, either. She worked for Erica in the morning, then gave Belle a bath, washed the curtains, cleaned the windows, scrubbed the floors, then went into the shop and reorganized the filing so she could be there if he rang.

He never rang.

Thursday she had scheduled up a daylong meet-and-greet chat session at the Moonstone with all of the island's artists, artisans and craftspeople. Lachlan had offered her the use of the front parlor and the services of Maddie, his spectacular cook, and Syd thought it would be an excellent way of getting everyone involved and making more one-on-one connections.

But by the time Thursday rolled around, there was only one person in the world she wanted to go one-on-one with.

And Hugh still hadn't appeared.

"He called this morning," Molly said when Syd stopped by with Belle on her way to the meeting at the Moonstone. "I'm surprised he didn't call you."

"I'm sure he called for business," she said, smiling, and doing her best to look unconcerned.

"He didn't talk business," Molly said. "He said he'd be in this evening. But then he didn't know about the storm."

"What storm?"

It was a clear blue sky as far as Syd could see. Hotter and muggier than yesterday, and even more than the day before, but this was August in the Bahamas. Heat and humidity were to be expected.

"The Storm," Molly repeated patiently. Her tone capitalized the S. "Obviously you haven't been listening to Trina. If you're going to be a real islander, Syd, you've got to pay attention to Trina."

Trina was the "weather girl" on the local radio station. More than that she was a local legend because, Syd had been told, she predicted the weather better than the U.S. National Weather Service and the Bahamian Service both.

Privately Syd didn't think that would be very difficult. She was reasonably certain that *she* could predict the weather better herself.

Now she shrugged. "I've been…distracted." The weather

had been the least of her problems the last few days. But because Molly seemed to be expecting it, she asked, "What did Trina have to say?"

"Storm coming from the east, should hit here this evening, moving on toward Florida overnight." Molly repeated the words as if she had memorized them.

"Sounds about like most days."

Granted she hadn't been here long, but she'd lived in Florida for three years and they'd had their share of brief tropical downpours that drenched everyone, steamed things up or cooled things off, and were gone in scarcely more than an hour.

They were not something, in her estimation, to be concerned about and, with apologies to Trina, she said so.

"Not this one," Molly replied. "Trina says this one will be a humdinger. They might even have to give it a name."

Syd looked doubtful. "As in a hurricane?"

"Well, those usually even the weather service notices," Molly allowed. "This one isn't really big yet, but Trina says it will be. It's gathering momentum. Should be here tonight. So when you finish up at the Moonstone, you might want to stock up on candles and water and batteries and stuff. I don't know how much Hugh has laid by."

Candles? Water? Batteries? "Are you serious? If you're serious, shouldn't I just cancel the meeting?"

"Oh, no. Everybody will be disappointed if you do that. They don't get invitations to tea at the Moonstone everyday. That was a great idea of yours, by the way, asking them all over there to talk. It raises the tone. Sets a standard. Says we're all in this together."

"We are."

"I know. And they'll be there. Besides, they're prepared for storms. And they know Trina has her eye on things. Don't worry. Lachlan will have the radio on. He'll let you know if you need to call it off."

Syd nodded. "If you say so."

"I do. Have fun," Molly said, going back to the engine she was working on. "Drink a cup of tea for me."

Syd started out, then stopped at the door. "What about Hugh? You said he was coming home tonight. He won't try to fly if there's a storm, will he?"

"Not if he's got a brain in his head," Molly said cheerfully.

And with that Syd had to be content.

Actually, as she walked toward the Moonstone, she couldn't see what everyone was worried about.

Yes, it was hot, but most of the days were hot. It was still, but that was better than windy, wasn't it?

Trina, Syd decided by the time she got to the inn, was probably no more accurate than the TV weather people. Once she was there and Lachlan began introducing her to people, she got caught up in the moment and forgot all about it. Molly was absolutely right. The invitation to tea at the Moonstone was a great hit. She met Nathan Wolfe and his wife, Carin, almost immediately.

They were both welcoming and eager to talk to her. Carin particularly made a point of saying, "I'm so glad you're here. I'm so happy for you and Hugh. He's a wonderful man."

"Yes," Syd said quite truthfully. "I think so, too."

I just hope he falls out of love with you.

Of course she didn't say it. She didn't want Carin feeling awkward. They chatted, they introduced her to their teenage daughter, Lacey, and their toddler son, Josh. They introduced her to other Pelican Islanders she hadn't met yet, including several that Lachlan had sworn would never show up.

Turk Sawyer, whose wonderfully creative paperweights made from island rocks and coral and barnacles she had admired in the Moonstone gift shop, never, according to Lachlan, left his front porch by the quay.

But he came today.

"My paperweights' been here. But I never been to the

Moonstone before," he told Syd, his eyes never once looking at her. He was too busy taking in everything else. "Reckoned I'd have a look round."

"Us, too," said the Cash brothers, Erasmus and Euclid, who made the wooden sailing ships and sturdy children's toys that Syd had admired when she'd gone with Molly to Carin's Cottage. "Pretty fancy place."

"I'm glad you're here," Syd said, stepping into her role as island development coordinator. This was going to be her future, she was determined. There was nothing she could do about Hugh now. She could do something about this. "Let me get you some tea or coffee and something to eat."

They shuffled their feet and shook their heads. "No, thanks," said Erasmus.

"Might get crumbs on the carpet," Turk explained.

"The carpet has seen worse than crumbs," Syd assured them. "Come and talk to me. Tell me how you got started." She ushered them toward the most comfortable chairs where they gingerly sat while she went to get them something to eat. "Is it true you only use local materials?" she asked when she came back.

They looked at her as if she'd asked if the world was flat.

"What else we goin' to use?" Euclid said, and Turk and Erasmus nodded. "An' where else we goin' to get it?"

Talking about that got them discussing their work. And Syd could see that they would have a lot to say in the right circumstances. It was just a matter of making them feel comfortable, of drawing them out.

"So what do you think about the storm?" she asked with a smile and a doubtful glance out the window where the sky was still blue.

"Gonna be a big 'un," said Euclid.

"Yes sir," Erasmus agreed with a nod. "Can tell by the way the leaves lift."

"An' the birds set," Turk added. "They be settlin' low."

"Birds?" Syd said. "Leaves?" She sat down and, clutching her coffee mug, leaned closer. "You know this? You're sure?"

Three heads nodded sagely. "An' Trina says so."

By midafternoon, everyone who came to talk with Syd about their work had also contributed to her growing lore about island storms. She'd heard how you could tell one was coming because the fish swam lower or you could tell because the reef turned black or you could know when the lizards' tails went purple.

And everyone added, of course, that Trina said so.

And still the sky was blue.

"Do you believe this?" she asked Lachlan after everyone had left to go buy candles or batteries or beer. "All this business about a storm?"

She half wondered if they were pulling her leg, trying to get her worked up over nothing. Testing her.

But Lachlan nodded. "Come here." He took her arm and drew her toward the window, then pointed at the horizon. "See there?"

Syd saw a smudged purple line. Above it she saw some grayish clouds. Nothing that looked especially sinister.

"That?" Syd asked dubiously. She wasn't sure what she'd expected. A little wind? Some thunderheads? "It doesn't look like much."

"It will," Lachlan promised. "Time to batten down the hatches."

Now there was a phrase that Syd had heard but never ever used. "Meaning what?"

"Bring in the beach furniture, the umbrellas, the potted plants. Nail down anything you can't bring in. Put shutters over the windows."

The only shutters Syd had ever seen were strictly for decoration. "You're not kidding?"

"I'm not kidding. Let me finish up here and I'll come and help you with Hugh's."

Syd looked again at the horizon. Was the smudge darker? Were the clouds closer so quickly?

What if Hugh really did try to fly home today?

"I'll go now and get started," she said, suddenly in a hurry.

Even though it was now neat and tidy, Hugh's porch was still full of things that needed moving.

Syd gathered up everything she'd been at pains to organize and carried it into the house. She brought in the bicycle, unhooked the hula dancer lights and the pink flamingo and palm tree strings. She put the surfboard in Hugh's bedroom, the dog bed in the kitchen, the snorkles and swim fins and scuba gear in her room. The various and sundry mechanical objects she lined up in rows in the living room. And every time she went out for another armload, she studied the horizon.

The purple smudge was getting closer.

Lachlan arrived about the time that the first gusts of wind did. He brought in the porch swing and the hammock, then set about securing the shutters. Syd did what she could to help.

She followed Lachlan as he checked all the downspouts. "Have you heard from Hugh? He told Molly he might fly in tonight."

"Don't you believe it. He's no fool. He's probably in some cushy hotel in Miami waiting for the all-clear."

Syd smiled wanly. "I expect so."

"He values his own skin." Lachlan set the last shutter. "There, now. All right and tight. Should ride out the storm just fine. Come on. Get Belle's dish and food and let's go."

"Go? Go where?" Syd shook her head, confused.

"To our place. You aren't going to stay here," Lachlan said, realizing her intention before she spoke. "By yourself? Don't be ridiculous."

"Hugh might come. If Belle wasn't here—"

"He'd know where to look for her. For both of you. Come on. Fiona's expecting you. There's more shelter where we are on the harbor side of the island. This place gets the view, I'll admit, just like the Moonstone does, but the harbor is where you want to be in a storm."

Syd shook her head. "I want to wait here." And when Lachlan opened his mouth to argue, she went on firmly. "You said it was okay. Right and tight, you said."

"I know, but—"

"Truly, Lachlan. I need to stay. I'll be fine."

She couldn't explain any more than that. Logically, of course, Lachlan was right.

But this wasn't about logic. It was gut instinct, no more no less. The last thing she'd said to Hugh was, *I'm not leaving.*

So she wasn't.

"He isn't coming," Lachlan argued.

But Syd didn't budge. "I'm staying here." As she spoke she rested her hand on Belle's head. A wet nose lifted and touched her fingers.

Lachlan's jaw bunched. "Fiona will kill me."

"No, she won't. She'll understand that it's my choice."

"Yeah, right. Tell her that," Lachlan muttered, glancing out the open door. "It's starting to rain."

"Then you'd better go." Syd went to the door and stood by it. The trees were beginning to sway. "Please, Lachlan. I'll be fine. I said I'd be here."

He opened his mouth and looked as if he might argue, but then he closed it again and slowly shook his head. "By God, you're as stubborn as he is. You deserve each other." Then he gave her a hard hug and said, "If my wife kills me, it'll be your fault."

Syd nodded gravely. "I'll tell that to the jury," she promised.

Lachlan grinned. "Pull the shutters across the door when I leave. Lock 'em down. If the water reaches the mangroves, though, you'd better head for higher ground."

"I will," Syd promised.

She watched him leave, then pulled the shutters tight. She felt as if she were in a tiny well-wrapped box. Just she and Belle. The rain began to come down harder. The wind picked up.

Hugh wasn't coming. She *knew* he wasn't coming. She even hoped he wasn't coming because it would be suicide if he tried.

But she needed to be here anyway.

She'd made a commitment. A promise.

The wind rattled the whole house. The rain pelted down. Belle lifted her ears and whined.

"It's the storm," Syd told her. "Just like Trina promised."

Belle whined again and went to the door.

"Oh, dear. Please don't say you need to go out," Syd said, dismayed. Surely the dog didn't need to be let out now. The rain was bucketing down. The wind was banging the shutters.

But Belle went to the door and barked.

The shutters banged furiously.

"Oh, help!" Syd cried, frantic.

And outside a muffled voice shouted over the din, "For God's sake, Syd, open the damn door!"

CHAPTER EIGHT

"WHAT on earth are you doing here?" McGillivray demanded, looming, dark and drenched and furious, as he dripped water all over the floor while Belle leaped and bounced around him, barking with joy.

"*Me?*" Syd stared, her relief at the discovery he was home and safe—if not dry—overridden by her astonishment at his sudden attack. "What am *I* doing here? *You're* the idiot who flew in the storm. You're supposed to be in Miami!"

"I told Molly I was coming back."

"And Molly said she told you about the storm."

He shrugged. "I left in time. No big deal. Don't make a fuss." He dragged his sopping T-shirt off over his head. "I wanted to make sure the house was secure."

Syd, who found herself staring at his bare chest, was suddenly dry-mouthed. She swallowed. "As you can see, it's fine," she said frostily.

Which was mostly the truth. There seemed to be some leaks in the roof, though. A few drops were falling here and there. But that wasn't *her* fault!

And Hugh, looking things over, going from room to room, checking to see that everything was shipshape, finally grunted his approval. "Yeah, it is. But—" he rounded on her "—I would have thought you'd have the brains to go to Lachlan's!"

Syd lifted her chin. "I told you I was staying."

"This is no place for a woman in a storm!"

"And I suppose because you're a *man,* that makes a

difference! I suppose, because you're a *man,* it was all right for you to take your life into your hands flying back here and then running across the island when there was no need!'' Her voice was high and reedy. She didn't care. ''My so-called stupidity pales in comparison! How dare you do something so stupid? You idiot!''

''Who's an idiot? *I* was out 'wandering around' as you put it,'' Hugh said scathingly, ''because I ran into Lachlan on his way home and he said *you* refused to come home with him!''

''Then you should have known I was safe, and you could have gone home with him instead and stayed tucked up in his house until the rain stopped.'' Syd could do scathing, too, when she put her mind to it.

Their furious gazes met, locked, battled.

Then Hugh, still scowling, looked away. Abruptly he hunkered down to rub Belle's ears and talk softly to her.

As if he was glad to see *her!* Which no doubt he was.

And Syd, watching, felt her fury ebb, overridden by the sheer relief of seeing him here in the flesh, of knowing he was safe even as the storm raged around them.

She'd considered the possibility that her analysis of the ''love thing'' as she'd come to think of it had been wrong. Sometimes, in the heat of the moment, she knew that she thought things that, on further reflection, confronted with facts, she discovered weren't true at all.

The love thing was true.

If Hugh hadn't made it back…

She couldn't think about that. It was too awful even to contemplate. She wanted to go to him, to put her arms around him, to feel his body hard and solid against hers. But she couldn't. Not yet.

He stood up again, ruffled Belle's fur, then stepped around the stacks of magazines and car parts and snorkeling gear, to come Syd's way. She wondered for a moment if he had read her mind.

"I need a shower," he said gruffly, and passed her deliberately without so much as a single touch.

Syd stared after him. This was the man who had kissed her senseless? Had he slaked his appetites in Miami? The very thought almost made her furious all over again.

But she didn't think he had.

He'd been careful *not* to touch her. As if it mattered. As if the lust that had raged between them three days ago had not been sated. As if the fire was banked and still simmering. As if a touch could stir the coals and start anew the conflagration.

"Want me to wash your back?" she called after him.

WASH his back?

Dear God, that would be all he needed, Hugh thought as he let the warm water sluice over him and tried to get a grip.

He had so much adrenaline zapping through his system that if Syd had laid a finger on him, he would have lasted about two seconds flat—if that!

She was already under his skin, inside his brain, haunting his thoughts, plaguing his dreams. He'd spent the past three days trying to put her out of his mind.

She would want things he couldn't give. He told himself that over and over. Even if she wanted him now, she wouldn't want him forever. And she sure as hell wouldn't want to spend her life on Pelican Cay.

He knew that. So it was damned perverse that he hadn't been able to stop thinking about her for three long days.

Tom Wilson, who ran a retreat house for business groups on a small private island just off Pelican Cay, had several appointments in Charleston, Atlanta, Mobile and Orlando as well as Miami. He'd been delighted when Hugh had said he'd stick around and fly him.

"Thought you had a lady friend to get back to," Tom had said.

He didn't even live on the island, but like everyone else, Tom had heard about Syd.

And of course Hugh couldn't deny it. But he'd shrugged. "She's got a life. She's busy working for my brother."

"That's what I hear. They say she's really sharp. Knows her stuff. Very capable. Able to cope with anything." Tom had obviously had an earful. "Grantham thinks she's brilliant."

"Yeah."

That was Syd. Not to mention gorgeous and witty and curious and surprisingly funny when she wasn't taking things seriously.

It had been like that the whole three days. Either Tom had said something that made Hugh think about her, or he saw something that made him think about her, or he heard something he thought she'd like to hear, that she'd laugh at or smile at or—

No, he didn't want to go there.

He wanted to forget Sydney St. John—and he hadn't been able to.

He hadn't even been able to go three full days without hearing about how she was doing. He'd actually called Molly this morning for no other reason than to casually ask about Belle—and the woman taking care of her.

"Reckon Belle must be lonely," he'd said.

"Oh, no," his sister had replied. "She loves Syd. She's always with Syd. I doubt she even misses you."

Traitorous dog.

"They're both fine," Molly had gone on blithely. "Don't worry about a thing. They can come stay with me during the storm. Or they can go to Lachlan's."

"What storm?" Hugh hadn't heard about any storm.

"The one Trina says is brewing out to the east. She figures it will hit early this evening. But it should be all right. We'll take care of things."

"Yeah. I might come home this evening."

His mind was racing even as he said the words, figuring out what he needed to do before he could leave.

Belle didn't like storms at all.

Of course Syd had said she'd take care of her. But what did Syd know about tropical storms? Or nervous dogs in storms? She hadn't had any experience with anything like that. Once she learned a storm was coming, she'd probably even take off.

So it was primarily Belle he had come back for, damn it, and not Sydney St. John!

But if the first words out of his mouth when he ran up the dock and saw Lachlan jumping out of his Jeep by his house on the quay were, "Where is she?" he supposed Lachlan could be forgiven for thinking he meant Syd and not his dog.

"She won't leave your bloody house!" Lachlan had bellowed, outraged, over the rising wind. "She said she told you she was staying there!"

Hugh knew Lachlan wasn't talking about Belle and he couldn't deny the exhilaration that shot through him at his brother's words. At the same time, though, he'd been frantic, desperate to get to her.

"She's a bloody lunatic!" he'd shouted over the rain sheeting down. "Lemme take your Jeep."

Lachlan tossed him the keys. "Get going. Get home!" At least he didn't argue with where Hugh needed to be. "She would have been fine here with us. But she wasn't going to come. Not as long as she thought you were coming back."

Hugh knew how that felt.

If he had stayed in Florida, he would have been worried sick. He'd have imagined the worst. As it was, his heart was in his throat the whole flight home—and not because he was taking his life in his hands. He was worried about her, convinced that Syd would be scared, that—if she was even still there—she wouldn't know what to do.

But she hadn't been scared. She'd been fine. She'd been

capable. She'd coped. Exactly like everyone said she would.

He was the one who'd been frantic. Panicked. Desperate.

He was still desperate, Hugh thought grimly. And no better off than when he had left three days ago. Worse, if possible. Wanting her still.

Gritting his teeth, he deliberately shut off the hot water tap and cursed as pure cold water engulfed him.

Still, it was a hell of a lot safer than letting Sydney St. John wash his back!

"THE roof leaks." Syd announced.

"Uh-huh." It had been leaking for the past three hours. Longer probably. The house needed a new roof. Not exactly news.

Hugh went back to his magazine and pretended to read. It was a six-month-old issue of *Charter Captain* and he had read every word of it at least three times *before* he'd picked it up this evening.

But it was better than the alternative, which was further contact with Sydney St. John.

His body still hadn't forgiven him for the cold shower. It didn't want anything to do with any further occasions for possible icy drenchings. So ever since he'd emerged from the bathroom, he'd been careful to keep his distance.

It hadn't been easy.

While he was in the shower, she'd heated up some conch chowder and had a loaf of crusty bread cut into chunks to go with it.

"Sit down and eat," she'd said.

He had because it would have been churlish not to—and besides he was starving.

While they ate, Syd had asked about his trip to Florida, to which he answered briefly and vaguely. If she was miffed by his stonewalling, she didn't give any indication. She simply shifted topics and began talking about her meeting with the artists' cooperative.

"I met Carin and Nathan," she told him. "I liked them both."

"They're likeable people."

"She's very nice."

He lifted his gaze and stared at her. And was gratified to see a flush rise above her collar. "I'm glad you think so," he said politely.

"I thought they all were," she told him. "Very interesting, too."

If he wondered how she would do with some of the more eccentric and crotchety members of the Pelican Cay community, he had his answer pretty quick.

She told him all about her conversation with the Cash brothers and Turk Sawyer.

"I didn't know they had conversations," Hugh said before he could stop himself. The only "conversations" he'd ever had with Turk and the Cashes in the past twenty years had consisted of his observations and their grunted responses or his asking a question and their saying, yeah, no or dunno.

But Syd had apparently tapped their conversational wellspring.

They told her all about how they knew a storm was coming, about what they expected to find on the beach after, how they would use it in their work and how they got started in the first place.

"They told you all that? Hell, they must have talked your leg off!"

"I was just interested," she said, "and they knew it. I'm sure they won't want to discuss their work with large groups," she added. "But given the right facilitator, I think they could be persuaded to talk with a few interested people."

"You could probably persuade pigs to fly, too," Hugh muttered.

Syd simply laughed. "Thank you."

It hadn't been intended as a compliment. Not exactly.

Though he was reluctantly impressed by her ability to deal with virtually everyone. What it meant, as far as he could see, was that she would soon be looking around for greater challenges—challenges she would never find on Pelican Cay.

"Then you can leave all that much sooner."

She recoiled as if he'd slapped her.

Damn it all, anyway. He shoved his chair away from the table and carried his dishes to the sink.

"Leave them. I'll wash them," Syd said.

He didn't volunteer to dry them. He just said, "Go for it," and retreated to the far end of the room.

It was where he still was two hours later, even though Syd had long since finished the dishes and was prowling around the house, straightening some things and rearranging other things, moving bowls and pots and such, and passing through his line of vision, distracting him so often that he was having to read the same sentence ten and fifteen times—and even then his brain was more interested in watching her.

"We're running out of pans and pots and bowls," she complained now.

Hugh grunted and tried to focus again on the article on new customs regulations. It might as well have been in Greek.

Syd emptied the frying pan from under the leak by the door and replaced it noisily. "I would think," she said after a moment, her tone one of consummate politeness, "that as you take such good care of your equipment, you would pay equal attention to your home."

Goaded finally to at least look up, Hugh saw her with her head cocked, watching him. There was a spark in her eyes that nearly had him looking away again.

Somehow he couldn't quite manage it.

"You would think that," he agreed casually, determined not to be drawn further into whatever was sparking to life between them. An almost tangible electricity crackled in the air, like the storm but personal. Very personal.

Hugh dropped his gaze to the magazine again.

HE FELT it, Syd was sure.

It was there in his gaze.

Every time his eyes connected with hers, however briefly, the electricity was stronger than any lightning storm. And yet he resisted it. Because he didn't want to feel it? Because he didn't want to acknowledge how good they could be together?

It was, she reflected, a lot like the merger that had just taken place between St. John's and Butler Instruments. It had made good economic sense. They were complementary companies. They didn't compete, and together they would have greater advantages than either had alone.

But Carl Teasdale, the managing director of Butler Instruments, hadn't seen that at first.

"Why would we want to get tied into a stateside firm?" he'd demanded. "We have our autonomy, our financial independence. We don't need you."

"You don't," Syd had agreed. "But we'd be better together. You'd have larger markets. More options. Better connections. And we'd have an international base. Let's take a look at a couple of scenarios, shall we?"

So while Roland had taken the CEO out sport fishing, Syd had shown Carl why in one scenario after another a merger between St. John's and Butler would be a good idea.

She'd done her homework. She knew what Carl thought was important, what he would respond to. What would Hugh McGillivray respond to?.

The rain still drummed on the roof—or leaked through—and the wind still rattled the windows and banged the shutters. The lights flickered.

"Let's play cards," she suggested

Hugh looked up slowly from the magazine he hadn't

turned a page in for the last twenty minutes. "What sort of cards?"

She lifted a brow. "Strip poker?"

His jaw dropped, then almost immediately snapped shut again. His whole body tensed and his fingers crumpled the magazine in their grasp.

"Right," he said, his voice strained. "Sure." And with careful deliberation he smoothed out the pages of the magazine and stared at them again.

"So, okay. We won't play strip poker," Syd said lightly. Obviously she'd moved a bit too fast. So now she'd have to back up, soothe his ruffled feathers, calm him down. And try again. "Gin?"

He didn't even look up. "No."

"Twenty-one?"

"No."

"Five-card stud?" She could see a muscle tick in his temple.

"I don't want to play cards, Sydney," he said through his teeth. He kept his gaze firmly on the page.

"Fine." Syd got up and went over to where the stack of magazines were in front of his chair. "If you're going to read, I will, too." She bent down to pick through them.

It wasn't her fault her hair tumbled forward and brushed against his bare knee, was it? Of course not. It was gravity, pure and simple. And when he lifted his gaze to glare at her and found himself staring down the neck of her scoop-necked T-shirt, that was his fault not hers.

All the same, it was gratifying to hear him suck in a sharp breath. And even more so to see that his knuckles were white. Interestingly, even his bare toes seemed to be clenched.

"Something wrong?" Syd lifted her head to inquire solicitously. Her face was barely a foot from his.

He was absolutely rigid, not even breathing. But she was near enough that she could see the pulse tick at the base of his throat. Then he swallowed. "Nothing's wrong," he said, his tone strangled.

"Good." She smiled again, took her time picking out one of the magazines, finally chose one at random and retreated to the chair a few feet away. She settled in and began to leaf through it. Out of the corner of her eye she saw Hugh flex his fingers, crack his knuckles, take one, and then another, deep careful breath.

The lights dimmed briefly and one of the shutters began to tremble. Belle got up off the rug and came to rest her head on Syd's knee. Syd soothed her, twining her fingers in the dog's thick soft hair, kneading and stroking and murmuring soothing words to her, then bending down to kiss the top of Belle's head. Outside the storm raged and inside Hugh twitched and fidgeted in his chair, turned one page and ten minutes later another.

He might have read all night if the lights hadn't gone out.

"Well, so much for reading," Syd said cheerfully, lighting the candles she'd gotten from Lachlan. "How about a game of chess?"

There had been a chess set gathering dust on one of the high shelves in the living room when she'd cleaned and sorted things out. She'd never seen Hugh touch it, but he must know the rules. "Or is it just artful clutter?"

Hugh's eyes narrowed in the candlelight. "No," he said slowly. He hesitated for a second. "I play."

"Play me."

Again he hesitated, as if he were weighing serious considerations.

Syd raised one brow and smiled slightly. "Or maybe you know you wouldn't win."

He went for the bait, like a trout for a fly. "Fine. We'll play."

"For stakes?"

"We're not playing strip chess."

"Of course not. I just thought we could have some stakes to make it more interesting." She smiled again.

Hugh gave her a steely, sceptical look, but he went and got the board and the pieces and carried them to the kitchen table. Syd set out two candles to light the game.

"Interesting like what?" he asked, arranging the chess-men on the board.

She shrugged lightly. "Up to you. If you win, you get to choose. What do you want?"

"What do you mean, what do I want?"

"It's hardly a trick question, McGillivray. It's very straightforward. If you beat me, you get what you want. If I beat you, I get what I want."

"Anything I want?"

"Anything," she said promptly, because it didn't matter. He wasn't going to win. She hadn't been a tournament chess champion for nothing. "Anything you want. As long as it's legal."

"Okay," he said slowly. "If I win, you put my stuff back the way you found it."

"Turn it back into a disaster area, you mean?"

"I mean give me my life back."

Syd gave a long-suffering sigh. "All right. Yes."

Hugh nodded, satisfied, and sat down at the table and waited until Syd sat opposite him. "And on the slim chance that you win, Ms. St. John," he said, a grin quirking the corner of his mouth, "what is your heart's desire?"

"I want you to make love with me."

CHAPTER NINE

HE STARED at her. "Very funny."

"I mean it. If I win, I want you to—"

"I heard what you said, Syd. Don't be a tease."

"I'm not teasing. I'm perfectly serious."

"Well, forget it. It's not going to happen."

"Not if you beat me," she agreed blithely.

Hugh glared. His fingers drummed on the tabletop.

Syd only shrugged, knowing she could afford to be magnanimous. "You can open," she offered.

He raised a brow. "No ladies first?" he asked snidely.

"I don't intend to play like a lady," Syd informed him.

"Why am I not surprised?"

She grinned. "You could concede now. Save time."

His teeth came together, and she saw a muscle tick in his jaw. "Fine, I'll open," he said, and reaching for his knight, he set it in front of his row of pawns.

Syd stared at it, then at him. "Are you sure you've played chess before?"

He met her gaze. His eyes glittered in the candlelight. "I said I had."

"Yes, but—"

"Having second thoughts? Worried now? Afraid?" White teeth flashed in a grin.

"Of course not!" she said haughtily. "I just don't want to demoralize you."

Hugh smiled slightly and lounged back in his chair. His shoulders lifted in a negligent shrug. "Your move, St. John."

Outside the wind continued to howl. The shutters shuddered and banged. The roof leaked.

Syd studied the board. Studied his knight. Narrowed her gaze. Thought. And thought some more.

Finally she moved.

SYDNEY St. John played chess exactly the way Hugh figured she would. Carefully. Competently. Always assessing her moves. Strategizing. Anticipating. Considering consequences. Planning ahead.

Exactly the same way Lachlan did.

Syd was another goalkeeper, just like his brother. Always defending her interests. Moving deliberately, anticipating. Responding.

In soccer and in chess—and in life—Hugh had always been a striker himself.

He moved boldly, looked for openings, wasn't above a little creativity when it was called for. He played fast and seemingly without thought, only instinct.

Seemingly was the operative word. He thought—but not like Syd and Lachlan did.

The game progressed in stalls and starts. Every move Hugh made was swift, almost instantaneous. And a good thing, too, as Syd took time enough for both of them.

Whenever it was her turn, she contemplated the board, studied the pieces, frowned, reflected, lifted her hand, then put it back in her lap.

"Aren't you ready yet?"

"I'm thinking."

"Still?"

"Hush!"

Hugh sighed.

Syd pondered.

He hummed.

She glared.

He sprawled and popped the top on a beer then took a

long swallow. "Want one?" He raised it so she could see it.

She scowled and ground her teeth at him.

He sighed again and tapped his fingers on his knee.

She bit her lip and finally—glory hallelujah—moved.

Hugh leaned forward, considered what she'd done, nodded, and moved, too.

"Just like that?" she demanded.

"You'd rather I spent an hour staring at the board?"

"I'd like to think you're paying attention!"

"I'm not the one wasting time," he pointed out.

She bared her teeth at him. And then started—or stalled—all over again.

An hour passed. Then two. He got up and wandered around, checking the shutters, emptying pots, cracking his knuckles, while Sydney sat at the table contemplating the board, considering her move. Finally he went and lay on the couch.

"Wake me when you've done something."

"Shut up." She was frowning at the board, lifting her hand, letting it waver over the pieces indecisively, then putting it back in her lap again.

Hugh began to whistle.

"Stop that," she snapped.

He closed his eyes. "Whatever you say, Syd."

He could hear the hiss between her teeth as she went back to the board. He scratched Belle's ears and smiled.

When she finally did make a move, he came back and stood looking down at the board. Yep. Exactly what he thought she'd do. Without even sitting down, he reached out and moved his castle.

Syd couldn't quite stop the grin from touching her lips. Hugh picked up a magazine and sat on the sofa leafing through it, waiting. But this time she spent only a few minutes looking things over before she took a deep slow breath and let it out as she reached out to move her bishop to block his castle.

Then she settled back and smiled beatifically up at him. "Check."

Hugh set down the magazine and ambled over to look at the board. Then at her. She looked back, smiling.

He sat down, then reached out and slid his queen over three spaces, took his hand away and lifted his gaze to hers, to watch her smile fade as realization dawned.

"Checkmate," he said.

WAY to go, moron, Hugh congratulated himself grimly. *You won.*

Won what?

A night in his bed by himself?

Whoopee.

No, damn it, he thought savagely. He was getting his old life back!

That was what he'd won. The freedom to throw what he wanted to throw wherever he wanted to throw it. The luxury not to do his dishes if he didn't want to, to dump his dirty clothes on the floor and his laundry in the chair. The joy of being answerable to no one. And of having no one care if he showed up or stayed away, went down in a thunderstorm or came in out of the rain, lived or died.

All the things he had pre-Sydney St. John.

The only problem was he didn't want them! And how damnably annoying was that?

He didn't want his old life back!

He'd begun to realize he'd probably gone overboard a little bit in the clutter department as a reaction to the austerity of his Navy days. And he'd been a little more footloose than he actually enjoyed. He'd begun to look forward to coming back at the end of the day and finding someone waiting for him.

Having *Syd* waiting for him.

He liked taking Belle for walks on the beach with her or going for a swim in the ocean with her, teaching her how to snorkel or bait a fish hook. Of course she always had to know how to "do it right." But the fact was he didn't mind teaching her. It was kind of fun. She was so earnest, she made him laugh and tease her and then she laughed, too.

And there was something about having someone care. Something about being the one special person in another person's life.

Hugh hadn't really given it a lot of thought until he'd seen the way Carin looked at Nathan. It was as if the world wasn't right—as if a vital piece was missing—unless Nathan was there.

Same thing with Lachlan and Fiona. Hugh had never really begrudged his brother anything. They'd always been good friends, but far too different to be competitive. But Lachlan was vital to Fiona, and it only took one glance to see that. Wherever she was, she wanted him there.

Sometimes, Hugh dared to think, Syd had looked at him like that. Sometimes when he came around the corner of the house after work, he would spot her sitting on the porch swing, and the moment she saw him coming, her eyes would simply light right up. She would smile and come to meet him. And then she would tell him about whatever new organizational structure she'd created to plague him and complicate his life.

"So you're well off without her," he told himself again, lying on the bed staring at the ceiling, listening to the wind howl and the rain drum down.

And it was true, damn it. She was Sydney St. John, mover and shaker, corporate hotshot, woman of many talents. And no matter what she'd been saying and no matter what she accomplished on Pelican Cay, she wasn't going to stay.

However she might smile at him now, she wasn't going to smile forever.

She was here for a reason—to learn to be her own person. Not her daddy's daughter. Not Roland Carruthers's useful-to-the-business wife. She'd stayed on the island to prove that she could do things on her own.

And she was doing it.

Which was probably why she wanted him to make love to her.

Just one more way to prove herself?

To show that she could get what she wanted?

Hugh's fingers tightened on the sheet. He twisted restlessly, trying to think.

But his brain was worn-out. He'd expended his entire capacity for thought playing chess. He had no cognitive ability left. Only instinct.

And his instinct knew just one thing: he wanted her.

THERE was a leak over her bed.

That was why there was moisture on her face.

It had nothing to do with the mortification of laying her heart, not to mention her *body,* on the line—and *losing!*—to Hugh McGillivray, who had obviously been so appalled at the thought of having to make love to her that he'd somehow managed to win the game!

Syd still couldn't work out how he'd done it. Not analytically.

His play had been so unorthodox she'd been completely confounded. How could you defend against a completely unsystematic attack? He hadn't had a plan, she was sure. He'd had sheer blind luck.

And she'd been humiliated.

She'd put a good face on it. She might not have spoken for a full minute, but when she had, her voice had seemed quite steady.

"Congratulations," she'd said. She'd even managed a polite smile, and then she'd got up and started toward his bedroom.

"Where are you going?"

"To get the clean clothes. I'll dump them in the chair. And then I can—"

"Oh, for God's sake! Leave them. They'll be back in the chair soon enough. You don't have to get them now."

"But—"

"Leave 'em, I said."

So she'd left them. She'd started to pick up the chess pieces and put the board away, but she hadn't done that, either.

Hugh wouldn't want it put away. He'd want it lying around cluttering everything up.

Fine. So be it. Easier for her.

Easiest for her to quit the scene entirely. So she'd given Belle a pat, said a proper cordial good night to McGillivray, even though she couldn't quite meet his eyes. And then she'd taken refuge in her room.

Now she swiped at her eyes and rolled onto her side, determined to force herself to go to sleep. But, damn it, there really was a leak!

And a squeak as the bedroom door opened.

"Belle?" Syd started to roll back over.

"Not Belle." The sound of Hugh's gruff voice shocked her.

She rolled over quickly. "What are you doing?"

What he was doing was crossing the room without a word. Then he dropped down on the bed beside her with such force that the bed frame shook. "You win."

"What?" She started to pull back but his arm pinned her down. "What do you mean? What are you doing?"

"I'm giving up. Isn't that what you suggested?" His voice was a growl in her ear. "You wanted this. You *said* you wanted it."

And then his lips met hers.

The kiss was fierce and desperate and every bit as demanding as the first one he had given her. And her own desperation seemed less humiliating now. In fact, she barely recalled it, consumed as she was in the sensations of the present—in the heated crush of his lips, the questing thrust of his tongue, the clear urgency of his body pressed hard against hers.

She locked her own arms around him, slid them up his

back beneath his shirt, reveling in the silken heat of his skin. She peeled his shirt up, eager for him.

And he jerked as if he'd been shot.

"Hell! What the devil—" He rolled off her and glared up at the ceiling. "Damn it! It's leaking!"

"I'll get a pan," she began quickly, determined not to let a leaking roof put him off his stride. He was finally in her bed. There was no way she was letting him out now.

But Hugh had a better idea. He was on his feet and scooping her into his arms in an instant, then striding out of the spare room and into his own where he laid her on the bed and loomed above her.

The candle in the glass on his dresser spilled a narrow band of golden light across the room, allowing Syd to watch him, to relish the planes and angles, light and shadow of his lean muscular body as he stripped off his shirt and shorts.

"Just so there's no misunderstanding," he said, his voice ragged. He stretched out on the bed alongside her. "I don't give a damn what happens. The bloody house can blow down. The Marines can land. There is no going back from here. I'm making love to you tonight and that's that."

Syd placed a hand against his heart and felt it thundering beneath her fingers. She curled them into the soft, wiry hair on his chest, then smoothed it, flattened it and leaned in to press a kiss where her hand had been.

Hugh sucked air. Then he rolled on top of her, straddled her thighs and looked down at her, his gaze hooded. The skin across his cheekbones was taut, and his breathing came quick and shallow now. Syd lay looking up at him, relishing the view, taking it all in, memorizing him from the intensity of his gaze to the hard muscles of his chest and the definition of his abs to the very blatant evidence of his arousal.

She lifted a hand to touch him, but he caught it in his own and held on. "We're going to play this the way you play chess."

Memory of her ignominious defeat surfaced and she frowned. "What does that mean?"

He smiled, his eyes glinting in the candlelight as he bent toward her. Just before his lips touched hers, he answered her in a ragged voice. "Slow."

They went slow.

Every move was languorous as he stroked his hands beneath her shirt, lifted it, then eased it off over her head. She would have unfastened her bra while she had raised up to permit him to pull off her shirt, but he shook his head.

"Let me," she said.

But he didn't. He pressed her back into the mattress, and traced the line of soft lace across her breasts with his finger, his touch light. It was like a feather, teasing a response from her.

She squirmed. He smiled, and then followed his feathering touch with his tongue.

"Hugh!" She arched up off the bed and fisted her hands in his hair.

But he didn't stop. He continued to lave her hot skin, his tongue dipping and teasing beneath the fabric as his hands worked deftly to free her breasts at last. So that when he finally did lift his head, the dampness he'd left on her burning flesh was cool in the night air.

"Tease," she muttered.

He grinned lopsidedly. "Just making up for lost time. I've been thinking about doing that for days." He settled back and looked down at her again, smiling his satisfaction at her near-naked body.

"You have?" She was surprised. Then curious. "What else have you been thinking about?" she asked him disingenuously.

"This." His hands roved over her breasts, tracing circles on them, coming closer and closer to her taut nipples. Then he dipped his head and kissed first one and then the other, his soft hair brushing against her as his mouth moved to press a line of kisses down her abdomen.

Then he lifted his head. "And this," he told her. He shifted his position deftly, without her even realizing he'd done it, so that instead of straddling her thighs, he was now between her knees. He was still kneeling himself, but was free now to caress her thighs, to run his hands up the insides of them, to tease the tender flesh there.

Syd trembled and ran her tongue over her lips, trying desperately to stay absolutely still, to pretend indifference, to deny how powerfully his touch affected her.

Until he touched her there.

Right there. Just there.

"Oh!" The cry escaped her without her even knowing she'd done it, until she saw him smile, then do it again. And again. And again.

He was stroking her, caressing her, opening her, stoking the fire within her. Making her writhe. Making her hips arch. Making her clench her toes and bite her lip as she tossed her head from side to side.

And then the stroking slowed, gentled. His touch grew lighter. And Syd clenched her teeth, hating the slowness, the gentleness of his touch. She wanted it deeper, harder, faster. *More.*

She was only vaguely conscious of the wind and rain now. The hammer of rain on the roof was nothing to the hammering of her own heart. The storm within was building inexorably. He was making love to her, playing her as if she were a violin.

But it wasn't enough. She hadn't said, make love *to* me. She'd said *with* me. She wanted to make love to him, too.

And so she resisted the storm he was unleashing within her, fought her own inclination to simply give in and go with it. This wasn't just about her. It was about *them.* Both of them. That's what love was—sharing.

And so she reached to touch him, too.

He jerked at her touch and his breath hissed out between his lips as his whole body seemed to tense. "SSSSSyd!"

Now it was her turn to smile.

"Yes?" Her gaze was slumbrous, her eyes heavy-lidded, but she watched him unblinkingly, learning his reactions, reveling in the power she had to make him tremble, to cause him to clench his teeth, to go rigid in an effort to hold perfectly still.

At first her touch was featherlight, caressing the length of him. She felt a shudder run through him and watched him clench his teeth. Then she curved her fingers around him, wrapping him in the warmth of her hand, making him swallow a groan.

They tempted, they teased, they touched.

And then simple touches weren't enough for either of them. They needed more. Hugh pushed forward into the heat of her body, sheathing himself in her, and Syd guided him, savored him, drew him in, then wrapped her legs around him and locked them together. As their bodies met, so their gazes did. And Syd gave him her heart in her eyes. His were so dark as to be unreadable.

But he never looked away. Never shut her out as he began to move, filling her, making a place for himself inside her.

That was it exactly. And Syd wanted him. Needed him. Welcomed him home.

She arched to meet his thrusts, wrapped her arms around him, clinging for dear life as he shattered and she gave herself up to the storm.

GOD in heaven, what a mess.

It was the first thought Hugh had—when he finally managed a coherent one.

It was at least an hour after he'd made love to her—and she to him—before he even remembered his own name. Right after their lovemaking he'd been drained, body and soul. He hadn't cared if the roof leaked, if the house creaked or if the whole island blew away.

It was all he could do to roll over and hold her in his arms, to listen to the thunder of her heart beating in time with his own and drift on the sensations still shuddering like aftershocks through his body. It had been the most incredible experience of his life—more memorable even than when he'd soloed in his first plane.

And yet...it was wrong.

Syd was asleep, happy for the moment in her dreams. He could see her cheek curve as she smiled.

But he wasn't smiling. He didn't know what to do next.

He knew what he shouldn't have done. But it was too late to change that now.

He'd been a fool to make love to her. But he hadn't been able to help himself. He'd gone to her because she'd goaded him, because he'd wanted her for days, because no matter what he'd done to get rid of it, the lust he felt hadn't gone away.

Sleep with her, damn it, he'd told himself. *It's what she wants, after all!* She'd said so herself.

And maybe that would do the trick.

So he'd set aside the very scruples that had kept him from taking Lisa Milligan to his bed.

He had made love to Sydney St. John for all the wrong reasons.

And for all the right ones, too. And that was the most terrifying thing of all.

He loved her.

Which meant that she was still in his system. Dug in deeper than ever. Under his skin like no woman—not even Carin—had ever been before. It was worse than loving Carin. Far worse.

He had never made love to Carin Campbell. Had wanted to for years. Or so he'd thought. But now he couldn't imagine it.

His mind had no room for any other woman. It was filled

with images of Syd naked beneath him, Syd in the throes of passion, Syd taking him into her body, Syd shattering in his arms.

He had never met a woman who had affected him like Syd. Never met one who had captured him, heart and soul, blotting all the others out of his mind. Loving Syd had made him forget that Carin Campbell even existed.

He knew now that what he'd felt for Carin had been a dream. The fantasy of a young man's hopes pinned on the wrong woman for him.

Carin had known that.

Now Hugh knew it, too.

He knew how different that was from what he felt for Syd. She had been in his arms. He had loved her. Still did.

He loved *Syd*. No one else.

He wanted *Syd*. No one else.

For all the good it did.

He knew himself. Knew his strengths and weaknesses, his reach and his limitations. He couldn't be Mr. Corporate Husband while his wife ran St. John Electronics. And even if he could, it didn't matter because Syd would never want to marry him.

They had been using each other from the very start.

She had used him to avoid marrying Roland. He had used her to keep Lisa from infiltrating his life. Tonight she had wanted him to make love to her not because she was in love with him but because it had been part of her emancipation. One more way of declaring herself her own person, free of her father and Roland Carruthers.

Just because she had turned her back on Roland Carruthers, that didn't mean she'd turned her back on sex.

Syd was a vital passionate woman. Who knew that better than him? From the very beginning something had sparked between them. Had it been chemistry? Hormones? An itch she'd wanted to scratch?

Whichever. Hugh had been elected to scratch it.

And that was that.

There had been no "I love you..."
Because she didn't.
He'd been a means to an end. No more, no less.

HE WAS so quiet.

Syd had never seen Hugh this quiet. Of course she knew he was exhausted. She didn't have to be told that his flight back from Miami had been harrowing, even though he'd pretended otherwise. And she knew that their frenzied desperate lovemaking had shattered her, so it seemed only right to expect it had taken a toll on him as well.

But she had slept afterward. She didn't know about Hugh.

Every time she had lifted her gaze to look at his face, his eyes were open. He had been staring into the distance—at the ceiling, out the window, anywhere but at her.

And when she called him back to her, when she whispered his name or touched his cheek with her fingers or pressed a kiss into his shoulder or along his jaw, he looked at her then, but only briefly. He smiled, but it seemed a sad smile, a distant smile.

She told herself he loved her. He had to.

He couldn't possibly have made love like that and not cared. Could he?

They had slept together all night long. He held her in his arms.

But all the words she wanted to hear, he never spoke.

And now, this morning, when she awoke, he wasn't there.

His side of the bed was cold and empty, and Syd felt a moment's panic, as if the memory had been a dream and the reality was that he hadn't come back at all.

But then she heard his voice outside, talking to someone, sounding easy and normal, and she knew it hadn't been a dream. And for a few minutes she lay back and dared to hope.

The sun was shining. The air was fresh. There was only

the slightest breeze coming in off the sea. She dressed and went out onto the porch to find that he had put everything back on it—the hammock, the porch swing, the shelves with the snorkeling gear, even the stack of magazines.

Exactly the way she'd had it.

What about getting his life back? Doing things the way *he* wanted them done? What about that?

She smiled. Her hopes rose a notch.

He hadn't seen her yet. He was shoveling hard and furious, his back already slick with sweat as he cleared the sand off the walk.

"Good morning," she said.

He jerked, then swung around, but his eyes were hooded, his expression unreadable. "Morning."

She almost said something about the way he'd put things back on the porch, then decided she'd better not. So she contented herself with "I can't believe how beautiful it is. Cool. Quiet. You'd never think that last night we nearly got blown away. What a difference a day makes."

Their gazes met—and though she was sure this time what he was thinking—that today things were indeed different between them than yesterday—she still didn't have a clue what he thought about that.

And he wasn't going to tell her. He simply nodded. "Yeah."

Then he turned and gazed out toward the beach and the sea, which now lapped calmly on the sand. "Turk Sawyer just came by. Wanted to know if you'd like to go scavenging with him and the Cashes."

"Scavenging?"

"Looking for stuff after the storm. He said he told you that they got a lot of good stuff that way. They're going out this morning. Thought you might like to come along. You can see 'em down the beach there." He jerked his head toward the point and, through the bushes, Syd could just make out three small figures moving slowly down the beach. One was pushing a wheelbarrow.

"Turk said if you wanted, you were welcome to catch up with them. They'd be glad to have you along." He looked as if he was surprised to be reporting such an invitation.

Syd was gratified to have received it. It meant she had connected with Turk and the Cash brothers. It meant she hadn't lost her touch.

Not with most people, anyway. She wasn't sure about Hugh.

She wished he would smile at her, wished he would lean his shovel against the wall and come to her and take her in his arms.

But she'd pushed him as far as she dared. The rest was up to him.

Maybe if she went with Turk and the Cashes, he would have time to think about what had happened between them. Or maybe he would ask her to stay and spend the morning with him.

"I believe I will go," she decided. "Unless," she added, "you'd rather I stuck around?" She made it a question, but she didn't want to hint too broadly.

Hugh shrugged and went back to shoveling. "Have a good time."

HARD work was good for what ailed you.

His father had always said that. So had Aunt Esme. The U.S. Navy certainly believed it.

Hugh believed it, too.

But hard work wasn't helping this time. Not helping at all. He spent the morning shoveling and sweeping and cleaning and reopening the shutters and doing whatever repairs needed to be done. The house looked great—better than it ever had.

Then he started on the roof. He'd bought the shingles last year, but he hadn't bothered to put them on because the rains hadn't been bad. Now it seemed like a good time to get to work. And from up there he could keep an eye on Syd and the oldsters as they ambled down the beach.

He'd been amazed when Turk had appeared this morning, voluntarily coming to seek her out. Turk and the Cashes might not be bona fide recluses, but they were very close. And yet Syd had charmed them. She'd talked to them about their work, encouraged them to talk to her. It was clear that all three old men were pretty impressed by her.

"She's got a way about her, that 'un," Turk said.

Yes, she did. Hugh was willing to admit it. She'd charmed him, too. Had brought him under her spell as easily and as thoroughly as she'd captivated the three old men and all the rest of the island folk.

More so, really. He loved her. He wanted her. He couldn't stop thinking about her, not even if he tried. He couldn't stop lifting his gaze to watch her as she and her band of admirers wandered slowly down the beach.

He could have finished the roof in a couple of hours if he hadn't kept stopping and gazing down the beach, watching as she picked up this or admired something that one of the old men had found. But he kept working, moving slowly, enjoying the view.

She looked so happy. Several times he saw her skipping in the foam of the incoming waves, twirling and laughing and, once, she'd grabbed one of the twins by the hands and spun him around with her.

Once, too, she had looked his way and waved.

Hugh had felt caught out, as if she'd spied him doing something he shouldn't. He'd pretended not to notice. But when she kept waving, finally he'd lifted a hand and awkwardly waved back.

She had grinned and hopped on one foot and waved gaily at him. Then she'd grabbed Turk and one of the Cashes and danced in and out of the foam.

Watching her, Hugh wondered if it might be possible. Could she really be happy here? Could she find enough challenges to make living here—with him—a possibility?

If she enjoyed something as simple as a morning on the beach looking for bits of driftwood with three old men, maybe—just maybe—she could.

"Is this McGillivray's?" The voice from below startled him.

Hugh looked down to see a stranger standing there. Middle-aged. Tall and fit, wearing nicely pressed white duck trousers and an open-necked blue shirt. His blond hair was windblown, but barely a strand looked out of place.

A well-heeled client, Hugh decided, who had got stuck on the island because of the storm, whose life had been put on hold for eighteen hours, and who now needed off this instant.

Which didn't sound like a bad idea. He could use a little perspective.

He smiled down at the man. "That's right. I'm Hugh McGillivray. What can I do for you?"

"Tell me where I can find Margaret St. John. My name is Roland Carruthers."

CHAPTER TEN

FOR a split second Hugh's world flipped upside down.

He must have looked as dazed as he felt because Roland Carruthers tapped his foot impatiently, then shrugged and said, "Never mind. I was obviously given erroneous information. Good day." He turned and started toward the road again.

But Hugh called, "Wait!"

Carruthers turned back, shading his eyes now as he looked up. "What is it? Do you know where she is?"

Hugh could see her a mile down the beach but he wasn't telling that to Carruthers. He stood up and wiped his grimy hands on his shorts. His heart was pounding harder than his hammer had. "I might. What do you want with her?"

Carruthers hesitated. Then he said, "I want to speak with her. Privately. On a personal matter. So if you'll tell me where she's living—"

"She's living here."

"*Here?*" If it was possible to look down his nose while looking up in the air, Carruthers would have done so.

"That's right." Hugh could look down his nose much more effectively. He did,' hands on hips, glaring. Their gazes locked. Dueled. "Got a problem with it?"

Carruthers took a step back, then pressed his lips together in a thin line. "No. I'm sure she's very grateful for your hospitality. I'll just get her things, then."

Hugh dropped the hammer, crouched slightly and, to Carruthers's clear amazement, jumped off the roof to land in the sand directly in front of him.

"Like hell you will," he said pleasantly.

Carruthers took a sensible step back and cleared his throat. He also eased the collar of his open-necked shirt, though it was hard to see how it could possibly be too tight. "Well, fine," he said, regarding Hugh with something between nervousness and irritation. "If you don't want me to take her things immediately, I'll just wait until she arrives."

Hugh hooked his thumbs in his belt loops and regarded Carruthers narrowly. If he'd thought Syd had exaggerated the man's arrogance, he did no longer. It was obvious that Carruthers was a patronizing overbearing jerk.

"Wait all you want," he said, "but I don't imagine she'll be glad to see you."

"I'm sure you're mistaken. I expect she'll be extremely glad to see me. I am her fiancé."

"No," Hugh said, "you're not."

"I beg your pardon," Carruthers replied, mustering all the haughtiness of which he was capable. "I don't know how you could know such a thing, Mr. McGillivray."

"I know," Hugh said levelly, "because she's married to me."

"WE'RE married?" Syd stared at Hugh, hardly able to believe her ears.

She'd been surprised enough to see him striding down the beach toward her moments ago. And his news that Carruthers was waiting at the house was annoying.

But the last thing she'd expected Hugh McGillivray to say was, "I told him we were married."

"Did you say we're *married?*"

"I told *him* that," Hugh replied tersely. "Obviously we're not."

"Obviously, um, not," Syd said, still feeling a little dazed. "I don't quite understand," she began tentatively, giving her head a little shake as she tried to catch up with him. He'd come to get her on the beach, had told Turk and the Cash brothers that she had urgent business at the house.

They'd winked and grinned and said, "Don't do nothin' we wouldn't do."

And Hugh had said, "Too late for that." And then he'd grabbed her hand and begun towing her back toward the house telling her he'd said he was married to her.

"But why…?" she began again.

"Because he thought you'd fall all over him with joy. Because he doesn't get it even now. Because he's such a pompous, overbearing, arrogant prig!" Hugh was stalking furiously back up the beach toward the house. Syd practically had to run to keep up with him.

"Pompous, overbearing, arrogant prig? Yes, that's Roland," she agreed. "But even so—"

"How the hell could you ever work with him?"

She shrugged. "I didn't hire him. My father did. And he is good at what he does."

Hugh gave her a sharp look. "And that excuses it?"

"Of course not. But it's the truth. Roland gets things done. He's a good businessman." She paused. "But that doesn't mean I wanted to marry him," she clarified, in case he got the wrong idea. "Did he believe you?" she asked just out of curiosity.

"No, he didn't." Hugh looked annoyed at that. "He said he couldn't imagine what a sane, sensible woman like you could possibly see in a bum like me."

Syd had no trouble guessing that he was delivering an exact quote.

"Sometimes tact isn't his strong point," she said.

Hugh shrugged. "Doesn't matter. I told him if he didn't believe me, he could ask you. In fact," he said gruffly, "I told him to stay with us while he was on the island if he didn't believe me."

Syd gaped. "You did *what?*"

Hugh's eyes flashed angrily. "A picture is worth a thousand words, isn't that what they say? I figured spending a little time with us in our house ought to be worth a few thousand." He muttered a few words that singed Syd's ears. Then he lifted his gaze and fixed her with a hard stare. "Unless, of course, you *want* to go with him?"

"Of course I don't!"

He shrugged. "Well, then...he didn't look like the sort of guy you could talk to. I think you already proved that."

"Yes." Oh, yes.

"How long is he going to be here?"

"He said he flies back to Miami tomorrow."

"I see. And in the meantime we pretend we're married?"

Hugh shrugged. "For one day. No big deal."

One day. No big deal.

Except Syd wanted a lifetime. A proposal. A wedding. A real marriage. She wanted Hugh McGillivray in her heart and in her bed and in her life for the next sixty-odd years.

And what did *he* want?

"Up to you," Hugh was saying now. "You don't want to do it, fine with me. I just thought I'd return the Lisa favor."

Was that all it was?

Syd didn't know. McGillivray's motives had never been clear.

Just one day? It was nothing. A few hours. A pretense.

But you had to start somewhere. Syd stopped as they reached the top of the path in clear sight of the house. Roland was on the porch, looking their way. Syd noted that, and didn't care a bit.

She reached up and caught Hugh's head between her hands and drew him down and kissed him. He looked momentarily stunned.

She smiled. "Just in case Roland is watching," she said.

ROLAND was watching.

He was suspicious and doubtful and clearly sceptical of Hugh's claim that they were married. But he could hardly call his host a liar.

And as far as finding Syd alive went, of course he was vastly relieved.

"You could have called sooner, though," he admonished as he followed her around the small kitchen like a herd dog while she tried to sidestep him and prepare dinner. "I was terrified, Margaret. Out of my mind with worry about you."

"Sorry," Syd said in a tone that said she wasn't sorry in the least. "I thought I'd make spaghetti. Is that all right? Or I can try to catch Hugh on his cell phone and ask him to bring some grouper from the dock on his way back from bringing your things from the Mirabelle."

That was where Roland had gone upon his arrival on Pelican Cay. Having traced her phone call to her father as far as the island, he'd requested a taxi to take him to the "best place," certain that he would find her there.

It had been Lisa Milligan, working at the Mirabelle's desk, who had listened to his description of his missing fiancée and had sent him to check out the woman living with Hugh McGillivray.

"*She* doesn't think you're married!" he informed Syd.

Syd shrugged. "Shows what she knows," she said dismissively and set about making dinner.

Roland watched her every move, shaking his head and looking somewhere between dazed and confused. "I've never seen you cook, Margaret."

"That's too bad," Syd said. "I'm actually a very good cook. I can do a lot of things you never knew."

"I'm sure you can," he said vaguely. "I always thought you were very talented. But let's get back to the point. We'll let bygones be bygones, shall we? We won't mention what happened on the yacht again. Now when you come back—"

Syd began adding spices to her tomato sauce, but she stopped long enough to meet his gaze squarely. "I'm not coming back, Roland. I resigned. Surely Dad told you that."

"He said you didn't know what you were talking about."

"I know exactly what I'm talking about. And I'm staying here."

But he wasn't listening to her now any more than he ever had. "You're upset," he said.

"I'm not upset. I *was* upset. I'm not now. I have a life now, Roland. You and Dad are just going to have to accept it."

"But you loved the work. You know you did. And St. John's is in your blood. Just because you're infatuated with some grubby bum—"

The look she gave him shut down that avenue of commentary. Syd thumped the pot on the stove and began to stir the sauce.

Roland came around the table and stood beside her. "Look, he's certainly very macho. And I imagine he can be quite charming. When he doesn't look like he wants to rip my head off. But he's what? A beachcomber?"

"He's not a beachcomber. He's a charter pilot. He owns his own business."

"And a nice little business I'm sure it is, too. But it's not St. John's. I know you were angry with me. You had a right to be," he admitted. "I was perhaps a bit high-handed in the way I arranged our wedding. But I know you, Margaret. You're far too sensible to throw yourself away like this. You didn't really marry him, did you."

The way Roland said it, it wasn't even a question. He was smiling, as if it was nothing but a joke.

"I married him. He is the man I love," Syd said firmly, and knew her words to be the absolute truth. Legally she might not qualify as Hugh McGillivray's wife, but in her heart she was as married to Hugh McGillivray as it was possible to be.

"Dear God." Roland took all of three seconds to shift gears. "It sounds as if he brainwashed you. If you did marry him, you can always get it annulled. If you married him under duress—"

"You're the one who caused the duress, Roland. He

didn't.'' She looked at him squarely. "I'm tired of talking about it. This is enough. Read my lips, Roland. I. Am. Not. Coming. Back. To. St. John's.''

He stared at her, then shook his head. "You poor, deluded woman.''

She ignored him after that.

He rabbited on about the bright and wonderful future of St. John's. He told her she was wasting her education, squandering her talents, would never be happy here. And she fixed a salad and set the table and all the while he talked.

"You'll miss the challenge,'' he insisted. "You love it. You need it.''

But not like she needed Hugh. Not like she needed to belong, to be a part of a family where people really took the time to love and understand each other.

"Do you want French bread with your spaghetti, Roland?'' she asked.

"Oh, for heaven's sake,'' he sputtered, exasperated. "There's no talking to you! I was afraid of this. Fine. Have your revenge. Take a week. Take two. Take a month. But think about what you're throwing away. Then don't do it. I'll cover for you with your father.''

Syd shut her eyes and counted to a hundred. There was no arguing with him. No talking to him. No point at all.

Thank God at that moment Hugh came in. "Got your gear,'' he said to Roland, hoisting an artfully distressed leather suitcase. "I'll just put this in the spare room.'' But first he deliberately detoured through the kitchen, hauled Syd against him and planted a smacking kiss on her lips.

It was done for calculated effect and she knew it. But it felt so real, so right, so perfect, that Syd fell into it eagerly. He tasted of the sea and the sun and a little bay rum. And she felt bereft when he stepped back. Desperately she searched his eyes, trying to gauge what he really felt.

He winked at her.

HE SHOULD win a bloody damned Oscar, Hugh thought.

Or if there were prizes for a guy getting himself in the

world's most untenable situation, he would no doubt win that one, hands down.

And it was his own damn fault!

If he'd gone with his first instinct, which had been to jump down off the roof and punch bloody Roland Carruthers's lights right out, everything would be just fine now.

But no, he'd had to be civilized.

For Syd's sake, he'd told himself, he shouldn't grind the bastard into the dirt. She wouldn't think it was polite. She'd find fault, tell him he was a heathen or a barbarian or some other damn thing.

Which just went to show what she knew.

As far as Hugh could see, being a heathen or a barbarian had a lot to recommend it right now. A whole hell of a lot more than smiling and being charming to a first-rate jerk all the while pretending to be married to a woman you knew you wanted and couldn't have.

He needed his head examined.

But instead of going to find Doc Rasmussen, he spent the evening sitting on the sofa next to Syd, his arm around her slim shoulders, toying with her hair and acting like he could hardly wait to get her into bed, while he made conversation with Roland Carruthers, who didn't want to converse any more than Hugh did.

That was bad.

Worse was what happened after Roland went reluctantly off to the spare room. Then he and Syd went off to his room to spend the night together. Again.

Now he stood just inside the door and watched as Sydney lit a candle on the dresser, then slipped out of her blouse and shorts and into a sheer cotton nightgown. There was no enticement in her movements, nothing overtly erotic or come hither.

But Hugh was definitely enticed.

He wanted her every bit as badly now as he had last

night. Knew he would want her tomorrow and the day after that and the day after that with the very same hunger.

She was in his blood. Forever. And nothing he could do would change that.

He ought to just ask her to marry him.

She might even say yes.

She might figure she owed him since he'd saved her life and all that rot. It was the sort of bloody idiotic thing a proper, well-brought-up female like Sydney St. John would do.

But he wouldn't ask. Couldn't!

He didn't want any part of a marriage based on gratitude or etiquette or anything other than love!

"Are you coming to bed," Syd asked softly, "or are you just going to hold up the door all night?"

Hugh jerked, then ran his tongue over his lips at the sight of her. She was sitting in his bed, smiling expectantly at him, her hair loose, cascading over creamy shoulders, her breasts covered by soft lacy cotton, but still drawing his gaze, begging for his touch.

He took a desperate shaky breath. How in hell was he supposed to turn away from that?

"The hammock?" he rasped.

"What?" She looked perplexed.

"I can sleep on the porch."

"Roland would love that."

He gritted his teeth. "This isn't about Roland!" he said before he could help himself.

"No, it's not." She held out a hand to him. "Hugh?"

He swallowed. "Are you sure? I mean, last night…" He couldn't finish. He felt like he was cutting his own throat.

"Of course I'm sure," Syd said. Then she grinned impishly. "After all, we're married."

So be it.

Hugh crossed the room, tugging his shirt over his head and unzipping his shorts as he went.

If this was what she wanted, who was he to say no?

He'd want to die later. Of that he was certain. When she was gone and all he had were memories, the pain would cut him to the bone.

But not now. Not yet.

He slid onto the bed beside her and with his mouth and his hands and his body he gave her all he had to give. And she matched him every step of the way. Her hands roved over his sweat-slick skin. Her lips nibbled a line along his jaw. She tasted his ear, swirled her tongue within. A shudder slid through him. His fingers trembled as he parted her flesh and slowly, perfectly, she drew him in.

And then the world seemed to stop.

He rose above her, braced on his hands, and hovered watching her, learning her, imprinting the moment on his mind and his heart so he would always remember.

As if there was a chance he could forget...

She lifted a hand and touched his cheek. Her eyes were bright in the candlelight. A smile touched her lips. "Hugh," she whispered. "My Hugh."

He loved her then, as fully and completely as he knew how. He moved and rocked and touched and kissed. He drove her to the brink—and himself along with her. And when at last they shattered, they shattered together.

And after, as he held her while she slept, he knew it was true what she'd said: he did belong to her. Forever.

ROLAND gave her one last chance.

"You can get a divorce—since obviously an annulment is out of the question," he said as he stood at the back of the house by the Jeep, his suitcase in his hand. The color was high in his pale cheeks and he was looking anywhere but at her.

Syd smiled and pretended not to hear. She held out a hand. "Goodbye, Roland. Thank you for everything."

He looked perplexed. "What are you thanking me for?"

"You opened my eyes. If you hadn't pushed me, I'd never have known what I was missing."

He looked at her, horrified. "Don't ever tell your father that!"

She laughed. "Don't worry. I won't. Have a safe trip."

He hesitated and might have given her more than one last chance if Hugh hadn't leaned on the horn just then.

"C'mon, Carruthers. Move it."

Roland grimaced, then shook his head. "I do hope you know what you're doing, Margaret."

Her one-day marriage almost over, Syd stood watching them bump away down the potholed lane—the man she loved and the man she'd left—and hoped she knew, too.

HALF an hour later Hugh was back.

Syd was just finishing the washing up from lunch when she heard the Jeep's door slam. Her heart leaped into her throat. All the time he was gone she'd imagined how it would be—how he would come back and give her that lopsided grin she loved.

And then he would cross the room and take her in his arms and kiss her.

And she would kiss him back, of course.

Then they would stare into each other's eyes and Hugh would say, "That worked out pretty good, didn't it? How about we do it for real."

She smiled, her heart kicking over at the thought—and at the sound of his footsteps on the porch. She meet his gaze as he came through the door.

He grinned the lopsided grin, and Syd started to smile.

"That worked out pretty darn good, didn't it?" he said.

Syd nodded…waited.

Hugh reached down and ruffled Belle's fur, then straightened, saying, "Reckon we're even now. I'm going for a swim. Then I've got a charter this afternoon to Freeport. I'll probably stay over. C'mon, Belle."

He grabbed a towel, whistled for the dog, gave Syd a wink, and he was gone.

So MUCH for her ability to read people.

She was obviously no better at it now than when she'd misread Roland on the yacht, Syd thought as she prowled around Hugh's house, fighting a losing battle to control her tears.

She might be good at business. She might understand how to motivate people and get them to work together. But when it came to understanding relationships that really mattered, obviously she sucked.

It was not a good feeling.

And that, she thought bitterly, was the understatement of the year.

He'd done her a favor, paid her back for helping him out with Lisa and his family—and that was that. Obviously their "pretend marriage" had, in Hugh's eyes, been exactly that. A sham. A useful convenience. In reality she was neither girlfriend nor wife.

The only thing real about their relationship had been her feelings. Because, God help her, she did love him.

And she understood what he meant now about the island being too small for both of them. She had to give him credit, he'd managed to stay and live on the same island as the woman he loved.

But Syd knew she couldn't. There was no way she could smile and be cheerful and pretend to be Hugh's friend day after day when she wanted to be so much more.

If Pelican Cay were bigger, she might be able to handle it. But it would have to be bigger, she thought. Considerably bigger.

Like maybe Australia.

HE WAS a coward.

At three o'clock in the morning in a Freeport Hotel room, Hugh couldn't deny the truth anymore.

At three o'clock yesterday morning he'd been making love with Syd. Desperate, passionate, beautiful love. Love that, if he dared, might make his life complete.

And this morning at three o'clock he was watching old movies.

Very old movies. Schmaltzy stories with happy endings in which people faced their fears and risked their hearts and found the loves of their lives.

He tried to tell himself they were movies. Not reality. Fiction. Not fact.

But whatever they were, they were true. He *knew* they were true, not because he'd seen the movies, but because he'd seen his parents and his brother and Fiona, because he'd seen Maurice and Estelle and Nathan and Carin. He'd seen the truth in their lives.

When a guy finds the right woman, he does whatever he's gotta do.

Lachlan's words.

Hard to imagine wisdom coming out of his brother's mouth. But Hugh thought there must be some saying about in love even fools being wise.

Some fools.

Not him. Not Hugh McGillivray, who had done what he had to do—up to a point. Made love to her. Lied for her. Pretended to be married to her because he'd wanted it so damn bad he could taste it.

But he'd been afraid to ask her.

Because she might say no. She might confirm all his worst fears.

The schmaltzy movie folks faced their worst fears. And got rewarded.

What about him?

"WHAT do you mean she's gone? Gone where?" Hugh's voice was almost a shout. He glowered at his brother, who lounged back in his chair with his feet on his desk and regarded him as if he were part of the sideshow in the circus.

Lachlan shrugged. "She didn't say. She just came in this morning and told me she was leaving. Said she'd still help out on the island development, though," he added with considerable pleasure, as if that were all that mattered.

"The hell with your bloody island development!" Hugh snarled. "Why did she leave?"

"Maybe she got fed up with you."

Maybe she did.

Hugh slumped against the wall, feeling gut punched. He hadn't slept. He couldn't think. He'd expected to come home and sweep her off her feet, wrap his arms around her and tell her he'd been a fool.

Obviously, she already knew.

"She didn't leave any kind of address? Nothing?"

He loved her—and he'd lost her, without even laying his heart on the line. Now he felt lost, hollow, empty. Sick.

"Not with me. Said she'd be in touch, that's all. Maybe with Molly? Or Erica? Otis? The Cashes? Turk?"

"Maybe." Hugh straightened up, hauled himself away from the wall. Pulled himself together. "I've got to find her," he said more to himself than to Lachlan. "Got to…even if she's gone to the ends of the earth."

It couldn't be over before it had really started.

Lachlan, watching him go, sighed and shook his head. "I know the feeling. Good luck, bro. You're gonna need it."

HE'D said he'd go to the ends of the earth.

He meant it, but he hadn't actually thought he'd have to do it.

What the hell was Syd doing in *Montana?*

Hugh cracked his knuckles and shifted in the hard seat of the waiting room chair, as he thumbed through a magazine and periodically tried to venture a smile at the stern-faced receptionist whose nameplate on the front of her desk said her name was Dusty.

"Will Ms. St. John be long?" he asked.

He got a shrug for a reply.

"Thank you." He smiled his best please-the-customers smile and wished to God the waiting were over.

Then again, maybe he should be glad it wasn't. Sitting here, even while gritting his teeth, crackling his knuckles and waiting to discuss "merger possibilities," at least he still had hope.

Once he was face to face with her, she could say no.

He wouldn't blame her if she did.

He'd let her down. Let them both down. Hadn't been honest when it had mattered most. And now...

Now he'd been waiting, hunting, hoping for two damn months! He'd looked everywhere, tried every lead he could think of, but no one knew—or was saying—where she was. If Lachlan or Molly knew, they hadn't said. No one else had either. He'd asked everyone he knew. He'd even broken down and called Roland Carruthers.

"I knew it," Carruthers had said with considerable satisfaction. "I *knew* she wouldn't have married you."

"Then that makes two of us she wouldn't have on a plate," Hugh had said. "But I'm going to grovel."

"Are you?" Carruthers had sounded interested at the prospect. "I'd like to see that. I almost wish I knew where she was."

Hugh wished he had too. But he'd had to wait another two weeks until, amazingly enough, Turk Sawyer mentioned her.

"You still lookin' for your lady friend?" He'd poked his head into the shop and asked Hugh two days ago.

Hugh had practically leaped on him. "Yes! Have you heard from her, Turk? Where is she?"

Turk had shrugged. "Say she's in Montana." He said the word as if it were a completely foreign term, then shook his head. "Say she's runnin' a business there. Connections

Somethin' or Other. Found me a place that sells my paperweights.''

Montana? Connections?

It wasn't much.

It was enough.

It didn't take him long to discover that SJ Island Connections operated out of, of all places, Bozeman, Montana. The website said the company did just what its name implied—"connected people and products, enhanced lives, made the world a better place.''

That would be Syd, all right. Connecting people. Enhancing lives. Making the world a better place. Oh, yeah. She did that better than anyone.

Without stopping to think Hugh called the number and asked to speak to her. She wasn't in.

"Could I make an appointment?''

"What for?'' the receptionist had asked bluntly.

"I want…'' he groped ''…to discuss merger possibilities.''

There was a pause. A shuffling of considerable paper. Then the receptionist said, "Tomorrow. 11:00 a.m.''

Hugh had moved heaven and earth to make it. He had—barely.

It was 11:00 now. In fact it was a minute past.

SYD LOVED MONTANA. The local literature called it The Last Best Place. She was inclined to agree. It was beautiful. The mountains, the valley, the sky, the weather. It was always gorgeous. Always changing.

And very nearly as far from Pelican Cay as it was possible to be.

You can't get there from here, should have been the motto of both places.

That suited Syd.

She didn't want to go there. As much as she had loved it, she didn't want to be reminded. She needed a fresh start. A completely new place. And by sheer luck she had found one. She'd wanted a place with no ocean, no palm trees, no hammocks, no balmy breezes. Montana seemed to fit the bill.

Now, after two months, she was beginning to feel, if not whole, at least as if someday she might get there. She didn't have to work 24/7 to keep her mind from going back to Hugh every time she gave it any rest. She could go for an hour or two without wondering what he was doing now. She could sleep at night without waking up three or four times and wishing she was in his arms.

But sometimes, like whenever it rained, she couldn't quite push the memories away yet. Whenever it rained, she thought about The Storm.

Just her luck that there was a spattering on the windows this morning. Hardly a tropical downpour, but even so, Syd found herself staring at the raindrops and remembering, aching, swallowing hard against the lump in her throat.

She was glad when Dusty buzzed and said, "Your eleven o'clock is here."

Syd didn't know who her eleven o'clock was. Some man wanting to talk about a merger, Dusty had said.

Dusty wasn't the world's best assistant. She tended to forget things like names and phone numbers. But she was honest and reliable. She showed up every day no matter what. She also worked cheap. Until Syd had more clients, that was important.

Maybe, she told herself, Mr. Eleven O'Clock would be a wealthy client who could provide plenty of connections. You never knew.

It was a local connection she'd just made, after all, that had allowed her to get Turk Sawyer a commission to do paperweights for an art gallery on Main.

Now Syd pasted on her best corporate smile and stood as the door opened. When it did, she felt as if she'd been punched in the stomach.

It was Hugh.

Clean shaven. In a suit. Looking solemn and supremely gorgeous as she had always known he would.

Her heart leaped at the same time the pain did. So much for getting over him. One look and she knew she wasn't over him at all.

"What are you doing here?" she demanded.

He smiled slightly. "I came to discuss a merger." He didn't sound like his usual devil-may-care breezy self. She saw a nerve ticking in his jaw. It surprised her.

"What sort of merger?" she asked, trying to get back on a business footing. "Fly Guy and—"

"Wonder Woman."

"What?" She stared at him confused.

Hugh swallowed, grimaced, then met her gaze squarely, but the nerve still ticked in his jaw. "You," he said, his voice ragged. "And me."

Syd felt her knees wobble. She reached back to find the chair and dropped into it before she landed on the floor. *You and me?* She felt dizzy. Just a little short of breath. Did he mean—?

"Are you fainting?" His voice was stronger now, almost accusatory. Quite a lot like the Hugh she remembered.

Syd almost smiled. Numbly she shook her head. "N-no. I mean, yes. Sort of. I just— You? And me? As in—"

She couldn't quite finish because she didn't dare believe it. She wasn't sure she even believed he was here. She wished she'd thought to shake his hand. If she'd touched him, she'd know if he was real.

"Marriage," he said.

She opened her mouth. No sound came out. She felt like a grouper, mouth opening and closing.

Hugh moved closer. Close enough to touch now. She could feel the warmth of his breath on her face as she stared up at him.

He *was* real.

She closed her mouth. Dazed, light-headed, she shook her head.

He crouched down. "Why are you shaking your head? Are you saying no?" He sounded urgent, intent, vulnerable.

"No," she said faintly. Then she smiled. "I'm saying yes."

And then he grinned. That beautiful lopsided Hugh McGillivray grin. "Well," he said, straightening up, grabbing her hands and hauling her up against him. "That's all right then." His grin widened. He looked about ten years younger and a whole lot happier.

She leaned against his chest, looked up into his eyes, and knew the solid strength of the man beneath the suit. She brushed a hand over the fine-worsted wool. "Very impressive."

"I can when I have to," he murmured. He kissed her forehead, her hair, her ears, her lips. She touched his cheek and felt only the barest hint of whisker.

"You even shaved."

He nodded. "I'd have done anything," he told her. "I've been going nuts ever since I came back to find you gone. I needed to talk to you, to propose to you—"

"Came back? *When?* Propose? *When?*" she echoed his words, astonished.

"The next day! And you were gone! I came to my senses during some movie in Freeport."

A day? If she'd waited a *day?*

"I really do need to learn to take things easier," she said, kissing him, reveling in the warmth of his embrace. "Waste time. Not go off half-cocked."

"That would be nice." He grinned. "But hardly you."

"I could work on it."

"Work," Hugh reminded her, "is highly overrated."

"You work as hard as anyone." She knew that now. She also knew he did have his priorities straight. "But it's sort of fitting that you would come to your senses doing something as lazy as watching a movie. What movie?"

"I don't know. It doesn't matter. You matter. Only you. God, Syd, I do love you."

They were words she'd given up hope of ever hearing. And now, when least expected, here they were. Life was really amazing.

But she didn't have much time to reflect on it. She felt his lips, firm and demanding, eager and persuasive. And the truth was, he didn't need to do much persuading. Syd was all too happy to kiss him back.

The kiss was even longer and deeper and more intense. It left them both breathless. Eager. Hungry for more, but knowing the office was hardly the place.

"I finished the roof," Hugh told her with his lips still on hers, "if you'd like to come and have a look at it. See if it meets with your approval."

"No more leaks when it rains?"

"If there are, I'll fix 'em. And after we're married, I'll teach you to fish and to play chess—"

"I know how to play chess!"

He laughed. "You'll just have to prove it."

"Over and over," she promised, laughing, too.

Then suddenly the laughter was gone as their gazes caught, clung. Hugh's eyes were shining. "I was a little slow—" he raked a hand through his hair, mussing it, making him look more like the McGillivray she was used to "—but I got it in the end. I want to do this right. I love you more than life itself. The world isn't half so beautiful when you're not with me. Will you marry me?"

Wondering, Syd touched his cheek, trailed her hand along his jaw, then pressed her lips to his. "Yes," she whispered. "Oh, yes. I love you, too, Hugh McGillivray," she vowed. "And I always will."

THEY WERE MARRIED a month later on Pelican Cay. They did it right according to Lachlin and Fiona, who had done it there before.

The whole island turned up to share in the joy of the occasion. Erica found Syd the perfect wedding dress. Trina the weather girl promised—and delivered—beautiful weather. Molly was the maid of honor and, to her dismay, caught the bridal bouquet.

The reception at the Moonstone featured the steel drum band from The Grouper, who were later joined by the Cash brothers on the fiddle and accordion. By the time night fell David Grantham was playing the spoons, Simon St. John was dancing barefoot with Miss Saffron, and Michael the bartender was teaching Roland Carruthers how to concoct the perfect goombay smash while they sang "The Sloop John B." with considerable gusto. Belle was sitting next to Sparks the cat, watching the whole amazing scene in astonishment.

By the time it ended Hugh and Syd were long gone, flying to Montana where they were spending their honeymoon at a cabin in the mountains.

"No distractions," Syd had promised him when she'd suggested it.

But she was wrong.

The roof leaked.

Hugh, laughing, set out pans under all of the dribbles and drizzles.

"I'm sorry," Syd apologized, chagrined. She'd thought they could kayak and canoe and hike and fish. Instead they were stuck indoors.

"I'm not sorry." Hugh was laughing. "We know how to deal with rain, don't we?"

"You want to play chess?" Syd asked, deadpan.

"What do you think?" Still laughing, he scooped her into his arms and carried her into the bedroom where, mercifully, there were no leaks. He tossed her gently onto the soft feather bed, then dove beside her and rolled her in his arms.

"Chess, Mrs. McGillivray?" Hugh's eyes were dancing.

And Syd's were, too. She knew this game. She drew him down and kissed him soundly. Then she wriggled sensuously, luxuriating in the softness of the bed and the sudden hardness of her husband.

She smiled up at him. "Your move," she said.

The world's bestselling romance series.

HARLEQUIN®
Presents

Seduction and Passion Guaranteed!

Mama Mia!

They're tall, dark…and ready to marry!

Don't delay, order the next story in
this great new miniseries…pronto!

Coming in August:

THE ITALIAN'S MARRIAGE BARGAIN
by Carol Marinelli
#2413

And don't miss:

THE ITALIAN'S SUITABLE WIFE
by Lucy Monroe
October #2425

HIS CONVENIENT WIFE
by Diana Hamilton
November #2431

Pick up a Harlequin Presents® novel and you will
enter a world of spine-tingling passion and
provocative, tantalizing romance!

Available wherever Harlequin books are sold.

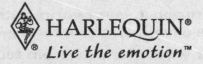

HARLEQUIN®
Live the emotion™

www.eHarlequin.com   HPITALH2